More

from a
Greek Island

Roger Jinkinson

Racing House

Best wishes

Roy J

ISBN 978-1-84327-942-6

Cover design: Electric Book
First published in Great Britain 2012 by Racing House.

The Racing House Press
20 Cambridge Drive
London SE12 8AJ, UK

Printed and bound by Lightning Source

For my Mum and Dad.

Roger's first job was as a cleaner in a school. From then on it was downhill all the way until he found himself helping to run a university. Already deeply involved with the remote Greek village of Diafani in Karpathos, the lure was too much and he gave up the formal lifestyle to live among the hunters, gatherers, fishermen and farmers who fascinated him so much. Two books have followed: *Tales from a Greek Island* is a series of short stories about village life whilst *American Ikaros* is the biography of Kevin Andrews, the American writer who came to the village in the 1960's. Roger promises that *More Tales from a Greek Island* will be his last on the subject. Linked by the interaction of man with nature this collection of essays and stories brings to life a way of existence unknown to modern city dwellers.

Also by Roger Jinkinson
Tales from A Greek Island (2005)
American Ikaros: The Search for Kevin Andrews (2010)

Contents

Arrival 1

The Village 8

Some are Gone 12

Not Easy 16

Georgos 23

How Georgos fell into the sea 31

The People of the Village 33

Manos 37

Going to the Doctors 40

The Turks 43

Death in the Village 48

Requiem 52

Going to Argos 55

Argos 58

Harri 62

To be a Fisherman 65

The Urn 68

Souvlaki 71

Reading the Signs 74

Birds 76

Balakas 81

The Boatman 84

Migration 87

God is Great 90

A Village Priest 92

Easter 96

Easter Week 100

Morena 107

Where do you live? 112

And then came tourists 115

Eleni 124

The Hirakis 126

Two Sisters 130

Some things do not exist 134

Frogs 137

Mantinades.. 140

Michalidi-Little Michalis 144

A seat in the Cafeneion 146

Every Corner has a Story.. 148

How are you Feeling?... 151

Weddings 154

Perfectly All Right... 160

Antiquas 164

Killing Eagles... 167

A Young Girl in the Village.. 170

Humour 179

World War Two.. 184

John Pyke 193

What makes you happy.. 199

Windmills... 201

Old Boats 204

Rembetika 210

Eleanora's.. 212

The Defining Moment.. 215

Arrival

The story begins with my arrival in a small Greek village on the northeast coast of an island in the Dodecanese. Since then I have been coming here for more than a quarter of a century. For half the year I live in my little pink house on the hill. From one window I see the harbour, from another the mountains. I speak a Greek that is unique to the village. We miss out d's, g's and several other consonants and throw in a scattering of Italian, Doric and Turkish words so that Athenians and educated people find it difficult to follow.

I have a small fishing boat with an outboard motor and I keep bees on the wild island of Saria nearby. I regularly dive to spear fish, lay out my nets or go line fishing. I was taught this work by my friend Georgos, an expert fisherman. Most days I can eat fish, but if the sea is too wild I walk in the forests and the mountains. Our priest, Papa Minas, used to be a shepherd and kept sheep before he took to caring for his human flock. He knows all the paths at this end of the island and showed me them years ago. When I come across an indentation in the pine needles with broken twigs and bent blades of grass I know Papa Minas has lain there to escape from the village and to gain comfort from the trees.

To check my bees or gather honey I take my boat and head north to Saria. I thread in and out of the rocks under the shelter of the cliffs, away from the strong winds and, where possible, away from the big waves. The sea is dangerous here. The weather can change in minutes – direction, strength and temperament. If this happens an hour or more from home it can be lonely. Coming back in the dark it can be very lonely. But the villagers are my friends. If I am going far I tell them. I make sure I am seen. If things get bad they will come in a bigger boat to find me. It has not happened yet. But perhaps...

In the morning I have coffee in Anna's *cafeneion*. In the evening I drink *ouzo* there. I time my excursions to avoid the tourist boat since tourists always ask the same questions: When did you first come here? Where do you eat? Is this the best Greek island? How much does...? Why? The only interesting question is: Why? But, they never listen to my answer. I try to answer it here because it reflects on the purpose of this book.

I was born in England in 1942. There was a war on, our tenement flat had been bombed and we were homeless. My father, an orphan at the age of fourteen, was away in the army. My earliest recollections are of travelling with my mother and a suitcase. I remember buses, trains, lorries, occasional cars, but travelling, always travelling. A few days here, a week there, staying with friends and relatives who did not want us and, even if they did, had no room for us. Poverty in those days was having no food, no money and empty cupboards. Poverty was bad teeth, anger, depression and violence. On D-Day, June 6 1944, my father landed on Gold beach at 11.25 am. His job was to lead the way for the invading armies, clear mines, cut wire, put up signs, kill the enemy - hard, difficult and dangerous work that occupied him until the surrender of Germany in May 1945. After D-Day there were the killing fields of Normandy, Arnhem, the

Ardennes, crossing the Rhine under fire, then a victory of sorts: a job done. He was a hero but turned down the offer of a Military Cross saying he had done no more than his comrades.

My father returned home from the war in 1946, but there was no home. Only a small boy frightened by this strange man he had never seen before and a wife scarred by poverty and homelessness. We lived in a one-bedroom slum with a toilet in the scullery and an open fire to cook Spam and dried eggs. I remember stealing wood for the fire from the streets and the bomb sites. I must have been five years old.

I try to imagine my father's longing for normality after the butchery of the war and his inability to express his feelings at what he had seen and done. And I remember my inarticulate mother clinging to the only piece of love she could understand. That of her only child.

My mother was mentally ill, agoraphobic. She was the youngest of four daughters with a younger brother, brought up in extreme poverty in a slum in Cable Street in the East End of London: one living room and one bedroom for a family of seven. The outside toilet was shared with three other families. Each child grew up with it's own phobia: Aunt Lil, a large woman, was scared of spiders, with Rose it was dirt, Aunt Dorothy had problems with sex and Uncle Ted was alcoholic. They were nice people and they tried to cope but there was no help. My father dedicated his life to caring for my mother. She made his life a torment. She did not have the words to thank him.

I left home as soon as I could and travelled. As a child I walked in the country, at sixteen and seventeen I went everywhere by bike, at eighteen I was walking and hitchhiking, mainly to England's West Country. My grandmother lived in Salisbury in Wiltshire before she moved to Cable Street. Using a pony and trap she collected herbs from the forest and sold them at country markets and

and sold them at country markets and Sixpenny Fairs. My great grandfather had been a shepherd. These were rural people, romantic and unknown, but touched on and described by Thomas Hardy. For some reason I identified with them and the search for pre-industrial life became my obsession. I had a folk memory of the days before telephones and mass entertainment, easy communication and monotone culture.

I sought different places and different eras: India, Morocco, Libya, Egypt, Iran, Turkey, East Africa, Mexico, Guatemala, Greece and, time and again, Spain. I was homesick everywhere, but for a home I never had. In Spain I met Socialists, Anarchists, Communists, workers and peasants seething under Franco and his indigenous army of occupation, the *Guardia Civil*. In the 1960s there were still parts of Spain straight out of Laurie Lee, pockets of life disconnected from the twentieth century, without roads, television or newspapers. I walked the old mule tracks, the paths of the iron hooves. In small villages or isolated inns I was made welcome by simple, innocent but suspicious people.

One scene is with me still: somewhere in Andalusia, a day trekking along a path in the hills, the sun hot and high, a white building across the fields, a cobbled road, horses. There had been no food and little to drink. I entered the inn and they asked if I had a horse. I said I was walking. They fussed and tutted. There was cold water in a clay jar. My room had a wooden bed, a straw mattress, an oil lamp, a nail in the wall and nothing else. The price, with evening meal and breakfast, was about 25 pesetas, say 20 cents. They showed me where to wash, after which I lay on my bed listening to life in the courtyard. I heard horses in the stable below my room. I smelt them as I dozed. A bell summoned me to supper. Fifteen of us sat on wooden benches around a large wooden table, helping ourselves to stew from a pot on the fire. And to wine. Young lads took me to a bar to drink cognac - six of us, three miners from Asturias, two bullfighters and me.

The miners were now *jornaleros,* day workers in the vast fields of the south earning 100 pesetas a day, or less. The coalfields of Asturias had been closed by strikes for six months or more, leading to pitched battles in the streets in the north with police and miners killed. The bullfighters were not matadors but fifteen-sixteen-year-old apprentices, travelling from one village *corrida* to the next. They fought steers and difficult, unpredictable bulls that the big names would not touch. They showed me scars on their sides, by the kidneys, ugly, red marks 15 or 20 cm long. They got their money scrabbling in the bloody sand for pesetas thrown by the spectators after each fight. Sometimes they got nothing. After many drinks I said:

I am *borracho,* drunk.

No, not *borracho,* only *tranquillo.*

In the morning they were gone and I had a hangover. The courtyard was empty. I drank cold coffee, put fruit and dry bread in my pocket, filled up my canteen with water and set off across an immense, yellow landscape.

Gradually Spain modernised and joined the twentieth century, tourists arrived, roads were built, Franco died and society changed. I needed to look elsewhere and I came to Greece. Crete attracted me for several years. I made friends in Zakros, a charming, small settlement at the eastern end of the island. I began to understand the Greeks' temperament, to appreciate their love for life, their hospitality, their faults and virtues. I kept on looking for remote, different places where the elements were important and had to be measured and assessed.

For several years I had wanted to understand the people and customs of northern Karpathos, drawn by photographs of women in traditional clothes and the strange, wild music. But the ferries were always a day early or late, or too expensive, or were cancelled due to bad weather. One day in 1981, with my family, I took the ferry from Pigadia in the south of Karpathos to Diafani in the north. It was late and the children fell asleep on the quayside. They were still asleep when we carried them on board. In those days there was no harbour in the north. The large ferries stopped offshore and Nikos Orfanos came out in an open boat, six metres long and powered by an outboard motor. We arrived about 2 am in a calm sea. We stared into the blackness. A voice called out:

Throw down the bags.

We lowered our rucksacks to Nikos who threw them to the bottom of his boat:

Give me those others. Throw them down.

They are not bags, they are children.

Oh. Pass them down carefully.

We did. Then we were in the boat, alone at sea in the dark, heading in the gentle swell to a small light on the horizon. The ferry, a floating fairyland, shrank and disappeared. My small son woke up for a second and looked around:

Are we going all the way in this?

Nikos looked carefully at the children:

You can stay with me.

For ten years we did just that. Now I have a house in the village and my granddaughter comes to stay.

We arrived at *to molo*, the mole. Nikos brought the boat in carefully, tied up, unloaded the rucksacks, handed the children up to us. We carried them, still sleeping, ashore. A woman in the traditional black dress, the *kavai,* appeared. She balanced one bag on her head and carried the others. We followed her to a little *cafeneion.* This was Anna. She had been waiting for relatives from the south but they had not come. She made us coffee while Nikos got our rooms ready. She would not accept money for the coffee. Electricity arrived at the village two years before we did and many houses had at least one electric light. But the hour was late, the village slept and, except for one streetlight, all was darkness. Standing patiently in the pool of light, was a donkey.

The Village

Most people in the Western world live in towns and cities. Many of them aspire to live away from the urban environment, they want to live in the countryside or by the sea or in a village. They dream of escape: a simple existence, being neighbourly away from traffic and pollution and crime: they seek peace in another environment. Sometimes they achieve this, but often they are disappointed: it is too hot, there is too much rain, they have moved away from their friends, they don't speak the language, there is no doctor, no public transport. She was fine until her husband died.

In the developing world the movement is the other way. Peasants move to the cities. They escape the slavery of the land to become wage slaves. They seek money, sexual freedom, education for their children. They want to swap simplicity for what they think of as sophistication. Sometimes in this new world they dream of returning home to their own idealised village the way it used to be. They want to go back to their childhood world with money in their pockets and stories to tell to those that stayed behind.

The village is not old, nor is it beautiful: the oldest houses date back around 150 years. Local people have little respect for the landscape and a massive interest in redevelopment and the few old houses that survive are at risk of being torn down and replaced by concrete villas with Italian tiles and aluminium windows. The location is spectacular. From Gabriella's bar, or Anna's *cafeneion* you can look out across the bay to the headland and see steep, pine covered mountains tumbling sheer to a wild sea. I pass under those cliffs in my boat, tucked in as close as I dare. Looking up I see huge boulders which, displaced by weather or earthquake, have plunged and skidded down the mountain and buried themselves in the sea at the bottom of the cliff. Sometimes I anchor my boat there, put on my wetsuit, goggles and flippers and dive to shoot fish with a spear gun. Under the water is a confused, panoramic jumble of huge rocks weighing 50 tons or more. There are caves too, home to groupers and sea bream, octopus and crayfish. Holding my breath I dive ten metres down, enter a cave and my torch lightens up patches of primitive plant life growing on the living rock: purple, mauve, orange, green; these colours are meant for fishy eyes, for monopods and cephalopods, molluscs and urchins. Where the boulders lie half out of the water and it is shallow I see grey mullet and barracuda. Where the water is shallow, there are shoals of *atherinos*, each fish smaller than my little finger.

There are three varieties of *atherinos* here, the fat ones are fried with tomatoes and onion in batter, the thin are delicious when freshly caught and fried alone. The third kind is neither one or the other and we argue as to how they should be cooked. *Atherinos* gather when the wind suits them and we gather them in our nets in the cool of the evening. This place is a nursery for the fry of big fish; thousands of them, every one perfectly formed, a bright, shining, tiny replica of its parents. When I am tired or have enough fish, I get back into the boat and wait to be dried by the sun. I look up to see large pine trees in broad hollows on the mountainside. No man has ever been to those places, but sometimes I see small parties of *agrimi*, wild goats, maybe four or five together. They are curious animals and look down at me with what seems to be amusement. In the steep places only small pine trees grow, scattered among the rocks like bonsai; a Japanese garden in

Greece, order among chaos. Up above I see Eleanora's falcons. In the autumn there are eagles.

Even these days, with the new harbour, the sea can exact a fearful punishment on the rocks and shoreline of the village. When a fierce *sirocco* blows from the south, ten metre waves can break over the harbour wall. From the east, when the weather changes, rollers come in, up and over the mole, over the road and into the bars and restaurants on the sea front. In the summer there are strong winds from the north. These are called, *maestros, trasmontana,* or *meltemi,* depending on their exact direction and they regularly blow at force seven or more for days on end. Tourists are surprised by this. They just do not expect Homer's windy island to be windy. The weather causes havoc with the infrastructure: when it rains or when we have one of our spectacular thunderstorms the electricity is off for days on end.

At night with a plastic sack over my head and whatever boots I can find from last year I run through the rain to the *cafeneion* and find its windows lit by the friendly glow of candles and oil lamps: instant nostalgia in a pitch black village. I open the door carefully and slide inside. It is crowded, for all the old men are here: having no light at home and with the television off they are pleased to talk about the old days, forty years ago, before electricity came. Anna makes *faskomilo*, the local mountain tea, or coffee, or sometimes pours an *ouzo* or two. She laughs as the card players take advantage of the low light conditions and cheat outrageously. Without electricity, without light, without television, Diafani is reborn as a community. Further west the twin village of Olymbos sits on the edge of its cliff with a backdrop of mountains, in the condition it held for more than one thousand years, pin pricks of light showing through the rain. Isolated, dark, broody and stern, Olymbos is the mother village: it was here before the other.

Community ties are strong and the villagers keep to themselves, wherever they are in the world they refer to Olymbos simply as *to chorio*, the village. And I do the same.

Some are Gone

The road did not reach *to chorio* until the late nineteen seventies. It is still not fully paved and the elements seem to think that it never will be. When it rains great rivulets appear and gouge away at the surface be it rock, gravel or tarmac: boulders tumble down the mountainside, bounce off the road and fly down the cliff the other side, or settle and form road blocks that can take days to clear. I remember one terrifying drive from the south with four of us in the front seat of a pickup truck, rain sheeting down and windscreen wipers that did not work. Lendakis, the crazy driver, knew we had to get home before the road was blocked. He drove as fast as he could, faster than he should, while I warned him of rocks and tried to work the wipers with my arm outside the side window.

The 40 kilometre journey took two hours as we careered from mountainside to cliff edge and rocks bounced on the bonnet and the roof of the truck and thunder cracked and boomed and lighting showed us terrifying glimpses of black rock and sheer cliffs. The road became a river, sometimes ten centimetres or more deep and I shouted, *petres*, rocks, as they bounced towards us and Lendakis slowed, or swerved and his wife and daughter prayed aloud and made supplications to god and every holy figure they knew. We were the only ones to get through that night: we arrived, battered and proud, to a candle and oil lit village glimmering dimly in the storm. Iannis Minatsis found us a fireside and I sat dripping in the warmth of the fire, eating goats' feet stew and drank hot, home brewed *raki* before going to bed. In the morning all was sunlight and birdsong as I walked down the valley to find Diafani scoured and gleaming white as it lay by the twinkling sea.

Has it changed, the tourists say, has it changed since you came here thirty years ago? My response is to ask has London changed, or Paris or Berlin? Is Hamburg the same as it was thirty years ago? Of course not. Everything changes. Sometimes for the better, sometimes for the worse, so why should a Greek village be expected to stay the same? For 1000 years the people of the village have been tough and resilient, fierce and enterprising. Since the nineteen twenties the dream of many of them was to migrate to North America, to Canada or Miami, or, in the majority of cases, to Baltimore. They went to other places too; Malaysia, Leicester, New Jersey, Morocco, Iran, the Congo, but the largest community is in Baltimore. Those that return, or stay in the village, follow a broad spectrum of occupations. A few are fishermen or farmers, others are builders or carpenters, plumbers, stonemasons, electricians, hoteliers and restauranteurs. Island people have to be self sufficient. Here in the village they can do everything. They built the harbour, the roads, the hotels and houses, they fix fridges, computers, cars, boats and outboard motors. Sometimes they fix the Common Agricultural Policy of the European Union. Just a little.

Except for a few women who run their own hotels or work with their husbands in their own bars or restaurants, women here have never gone out to work. They work in the home. This is not easy work, for the home includes the garden and the fields of Avlona and the olive trees scattered along the cliff tops. Women sow, reap, winnow and grind their own rye, wheat and barley.

They pick and press olives, bake bread in wood burning ovens, feed and milk their goats, cook for the family and keep the house spotless. When all this is done they sit, with friends: a circle of women who crochet and embroider as they gossip and exchange news and opinion. In the right season, or the right time of day, you will see women working in the fields, or fetching wood for the ovens. Then you had better beware. For sure you can take a picture, but you will be asked to carry this sack, or drag that load, or hold onto this goat while the others are rounded up. Then you will find that these women are nimbler and stronger than you are and when you look into their weather-beaten faces you will see there is nothing submissive about them: they belong to this landscape, they own the land, and it shows. They are open and proud, cunning and fierce, sometimes with a fine sense of humour. Don't cross them, you will bear the scars for a long time.

The people I am friendliest with are hunters and gatherers. Their style of life predates that of the farmer. It is not an easy life, nor a simple one. To live from the land and the sea requires a sophisticated understanding of the environment, an empathy and respect for nature. If you take too much this year there will be no food next year and you will go hungry. If you harpoon that small fish there will be no big fish. My friends hunt wild goats, hares and partridges and of course, they fish. They gather shellfish and salt from the sea, wild fruit, vegetables, snails and herbs from the mountains. In a glut they share their endeavours, at times of shortage they wait for something in return. These people and the shepherds from Saria are the ones that I spend my time with.

They have taught me the most about the landscape, the music and the culture, how to read the sky and understand the sea. They have shown me how to fish and keep bees, how to survive in a small boat in bad weather, where to gather wild food and where and when to collect salt. I am proud to know these people, maybe the last of their kind in

Europe. I have written about the village before and those of you who are returning to my words will be pleased to know that most of the characters are with us still: Gabriella is here and Minas and Georgos, Anna and Nikos and Iannis from Tristomo. Even Kosmas comes to see us from time to time. For his holidays, he tells us, *diakopes.*

But some are gone and their voices will not be heard again in the village, their laughter will not ring out in our narrow lanes and alleys. The village attitude to death is hard for an outsider to understand. The death of an old person is accepted as natural. There is formal mourning, many outward displays of grief and respect, traditions are adhered to and demonstrated, but the death is accepted. The old people prepare for their demise long in advance, their best clothes are ready for them to be laid out in, they are passive with an inner peace. Coming back after a hard winter I am fearful of the gaps in the community. One time I asked Iannis, a hale eighty year old friend of mine:

Did you go away in the winter?

To which he answered:

Pou tha paw? Where would I go?

before adding:

The truth is, I am waiting for Charon.

Let us hope it is a long wait.

Not Easy

What's it like to live in the village I am asked, what's it really like? Well, it's not easy, these are not easy people: they are hard, not to me, but to one another. There are feuds, some dating back several generations, some can even be traced to the social and economic standing of shepherds versus farmers. I am no longer surprised at the depth of feelings as I have grown aware of schisms within this small community: this person will not sit with his brother, another has not spoken to his sister-in-law for thirty years. Normally the feuds are properly contained, but occasionally someone will be called *hypocritis*, a hypocrite, or worse and then it gets bad. Not just:

You stinky old goat.

But:

I hope you get stomach cancer and it kills you soon.

or

May your unborn child be deformed.

These curses are thousands of years old, are meant to hurt and do. And then there is *keratas*, the horned one, the goat. Shout that or wiggle your fingers above your head and you are saying cuckold, the most deadly insult in a small community. You are telling some wife or husband that someone else is enjoying what should only be theirs. Inevitably, if you do this in public then blows will follow.

The old people take spells and curses very seriously. The priest asked me once if I believed in witches. I told him no and wondered why he asked:

> Well, A women who doesn't like me, walked past my yard yesterday in Avlona. She looked at one of my chickens, pointed her finger and said something:

> What happened?

> The chicken died.

What would you think if an educated, erudite man, well read and fluent in several languages, a priest, told you that story? Change the subject, talk about the weather? The young people may tell you they do not believe in such things either, but there are stories: chicken's blood spilt on the steps of a newly opened store is not good news. Neither is salt scattered along the route of a wedding procession: when it rains the salt will dissolve and so will the marriage. So, you need the right words to say or the right liquids to pour in the right place. Of course I don't believe in spells but, I took out *asphalia*, insurance. Even now, well into the twenty first century, as I write on my Mac computer, I look down and see my mobile phone. Among the messages I have stored away, in dialect, is what to say if someone casts *to mavro mati*, the evil eye, on me. Just in case. Just to be sure. And what should I make of a conversation with an old man in his nineties who tells me today is his 69th wedding anniversary?

> Congratulations, you must be very happy.

> No, I want a divorce.

> Why?

> It was a mistake.

And when I pressed further he explained that the skulls of women have holes in them, and pointing:

Where the horns come out.

Was I being set up? Was this dignified old man playing an elaborate joke on me or was I being invited to share centuries old beliefs from pre-Christian times? I really don't know.

Nearly twenty years ago we had a catastrophe, a terrible flood that filled the village with water in fifteen minutes. Soon after the big forest fire there was a violent storm with 24 hours nonstop rain. A gully became blocked by rocks and fallen trees at a place where the road passed, water built up and the rocks, trees and road gave way together and a wall of water five metres high hit the village. Fortunately nobody was killed, but it was close. One couple in their eighties were sitting in their one roomed house when water came pouring in. They climbed the steps onto the *pano sofa*, the old style wooden bed with storage space underneath. The room filled up and even standing on the *sofa* the water was up to their chests. The old man, Barba Iannis, was strong and holding hands with his wife, edged his way to the window. As he broke the glass, pressure from the water inside the room burst through the window and broke the wall and the old couple were swept outside on their own private *tsunami*.

The flood subsided as fast as it arrived and the old couple were left frightened, drenched and homeless, but safe in the lane outside. Another man, a little crazy, but a friend of mine was alone in the dark in his room. Water broke the door down, he climbed onto a chair, then the table, then the top of his fridge. His head was pressed against the ceiling with water up to his chin when it started to recede and he was saved. Houses were wrecked, gardens and olive groves swept away and mud deposited all over the village.

More than 100 people took shelter in the church, but the response of the village was not as I expected: there was massive family solidarity, but little obvious community spirit. Each family took care of its own, some providing shelter for relatives years after these terrible events, but some villagers had no relatives to care for them and their situation was dire. Of course, being from a different culture I behaved differently and with friends of mine tried to help where we could. Until we could steal a shovel we used broken plates and tin cups to clear old people's rooms of mud which lay half a metre deep. Of course we became muddy, but were surprised to be shouted at when we went to a bar for a coffee and a rest. Affronted heroes, we weren't allowed to sit down outside until we washed our hands and shoes and feet in the sea. Of course we laughed and so do the villagers when I tell the story, but it was a lesson to my friends and I.

Many comic scenarios arose from the flood: one man was worried about his donkey left on the mountain in the rain for nearly a day. He drove up the valley as far as he could, parked his car and walked the path in the downpour. He took the donkey to a sheltered place and came back down again. The car was gone: swept away in the flood. It was a new car and now lays in the sea, several fathoms deep. The donkey survived to a good age. In those days one of the Vasillis in the village used to wear a tee shirt advertising a German beer, *Lowenbrau,* so naturally they started calling him Loverboy. Seeing a storm was coming he pulled his boat out of the sea and tied it to the largest object he could find: a massive 15 ton truck. The storm came and went and Loverboy, feeling smug, strode down in the morning to check his boat. It wasn't there. Neither was the truck. After a few days the truck was found, buried several metres under the beach. He is still looking for his boat.

What I learned from the flood, besides a healthy respect for mountains in a storm, is that the village cannot be characterised by the cosy European cliche of everyone pulling together. Rather it resembles an interwoven, interconnected structure of close knit families displaying different tensions of loyalty and allegiance, rivalry, cooperation and competition. It is strong, but not united. There are two exceptions to this model. If you are a foreigner you will be looked after, protected and cared for by everyone. And if you have problems at sea, no matter the weather, the villagers will come to help you.

In the old days life here could be unimaginably difficult. I can take you in my boat and show you a small house on the coast: a beautiful spot, but a sad place. One summer, in recent memory, an old couple went there to prune their olive trees. There were no footpaths so they went by boat. The man felt ill, lay down in the house and died of a heart attack. He was a big man and his wife left him there while she rowed back to the village to fetch help. A storm blew up and it was a full day before they could fetch the body. Twenty four hours is a long time to leave a dead man in the heat and retrieving him was not a pleasant task. His family was a good family, his friends were good friends. They did the work without complaint, for there was no choice.

Another time an old man died in the village. He had been waiting for death a long time and was found on his bed dressed in his best suit. He was buried that day. As is the custom the family gathered to distribute the inheritance. There are strict rules for this, everyone knows what is available and everyone knows what is due to them. The distribution went well, except there were some gold coins missing. In the village such coins represent more than money, they are the accumulation of generations of hard work and suffering. The family searched everywhere until it gradually dawned that the coins had been in the old man's pocket. These are hard people, they retrieved the money. Look closely at the old people, you will see history etched deeply in their faces.

I can look at a simple thing in the village: a *panga*, wooden bench or a *skamni*, stool, and know who made it, who owned it and who sold it. I came across an old lady once, the mother of a friend of mine. She was sitting on an old *panga*, recently removed from a demolished house and crying. I asked why and she told me she had been born on that *panga* and lived in the house it had been taken from. In Wales there is a special name for the nostalgia and longing for home and place. Welsh people feel *hiraeth*. Here there is longing and belonging, a double dose of nostalgia that sometimes stifles me. There are customs, gestures and manners that take years to understand.

It is impossible to make plans in the village, everything is *aftoskedio*, improvised. I arrange to meet Georgos in Michali's restaurant, his son walks past, points in the other direction and makes a gesture of pulling a *sirti*, a lure, through the water. From this I gather Georgos had been fishing and caught *loutsos*, barracuda and it will be cooked by Papaelias and that's where the *parea*, company, will gather. There is no point in asking the time: it will be eight, or eight thirty or nine, depending on who is coming and what they will bring to the supper: artichokes maybe, or fresh bread, or cheese or figs. I wear no watch here. I take Georgos to his favourite dive spot. I ask what time I should come back. He points to a mountain and tells me to return when the sun touches the summit. This makes more sense than knowing the time. Twilight, or dimity as my grandmother used to call it, is the best time to shoot fish, so the sun touching the mountain is more useful than any o'clock.

It is not essential to abandon normal methods of thought, but it helps. If the sea is too rough for a *caique* we will take a small boat. If you feel you are going to die you get your best clothes ready. This is village reality. There are many others including the climate. One day it was around 40 C in the shade: at night it was so hot some of the restaurant owners stopped working, took off their clothes and jumped into the sea with their customers. Late at night the fruit wagon arrived, loaded with watermelons and an excited crowd gathered around under the streetlight. It was a scene from Africa. Children played in the sea until midnight and throughout the village I could see my neighbours going to sleep on roofs and staircases and balconies: the women dressed in white shifts and bloomers, the men in vests and grey underpants. When I got up in the morning I turned on the tap and there was no water. I understood how revolutions come about.

So it is not easy living in my village, you have to work at it, but there are rewards. The people are amusing and kind, they care for me and they show it. Half a loaf of fresh-baked bread wrapped up and placed on my doorstep in the evening, some figs or cactus fruit from Avlona given in handfuls, or a sack of artichokes in their season and always for my supper, fish. When I first arrived I was a stranger. Now as I sit in the *cafeneion* in the evening in early spring, or late autumn I can drink an *ouzo* or two, close my eyes, listen to the sea and feel, without doubt, I belong.

Georgos

Georgos was one of the young men I befriended when I first came to the village; Georgos, Andonis, Georgos Makris and Manolis; always having fun, chasing girls, diving and fishing with nets and *paragadi,* the long line with many hooks. I envied their youth, their looks and their freedom. One scene from thirty years ago is with me still. In those days I had a job, two suits and a secretary and soon I had to return to England to work. It was hot, even at eight in the morning, so it must have been June or July. I did not know their names then, but I saw Andonis and Georgos coming back to the village in a small boat loaded with nets. They didn't bother to throw the anchor and I heard their laughter as they drove the boat up the stony beach. They stripped off their shirts and still wearing their faded jeans, dived into the sea to cool down. Out of the sea they lay on the hot stones to dry, first one side of their bodies, then the other. They did not notice me, but that moment changed my life. I knew that was how I wanted to live and now, after a fashion, that is how I do live.

Georgos is a married man these days and the father of three children. Depending on the season and time of day he is a carpenter, woodcarver, musician or captain of a fast launch used for marine conservation. Always he is a fisherman. One of the best. We share a small boat, we work together and sometimes we dive together. Fishing with Georgos can be an adventure, or a trial, but always a laugh. The stories about him are many. Years ago, sailing to Saria to hunt he saw some partridges on a cliff by the beach at

Vananda. I slowed the boat as he took aim and bang, a partridge fell into the sea a few metres away. We moved slowly forward and Georgos lent over and with his left hand scooped up the dead bird. Suddenly with a whoop he plunged his right arm into the sea, reaching for the bottom. As he turned to me with a massive grin on his face I saw the partridge in one hand and an octopus in the other.

People here like to eat *patalides*, limpets, as *meze* with their *ouzo*. They like them fresh, raw and still alive. It might sound an easy job to gather them from the rocks where the grow and normally it is, but not with Georgos. It was a windy day, but his mother wanted *patalides* so off we went to Amoi, the little island just before Steno. To say he anchored the boat would be to overstate the action. He took the rope attached to the prow, tied a knot in its end, jumped onto the rocks and jammed the rope in a crack. I joined him on the rocks as the boat drifted in the wind, tugging at the extended rope and threatening to leave us stranded on this isolated islet. Armed with a knife and half a plastic bottle each and dressed only in swimming shorts we lowered ourselves into the rough, cold sea. We moved along holding onto the rocks with one hand balancing hopefully as we prised the limpets off and flipped them into the half bottles. Fortunately I was wearing plimsoles or my feet would have been shredded. Georgos, as always, was barefoot. The sea here is 10 metres deep and I was scared, cold and tired as I edged along, listening to Georgos cursing my ineptitude. Waving his knife in my direction he shouted:

Peerates, we are peerates

before telling me in a concerned, almost gentle fashion:

Beware of octopus.

Now, being up to your armpits in cold water, clinging onto razor sharp rocks while you look over your shoulder to see if your boat has broken free and drifted off to Syria is bad enough. Danger from octopus is another thing:

Octopus?

And Georgos told me something that had never crossed my mind. If an octopus takes hold of you, and sometimes they do, then you are held down not just by the weight of the octopus, but by the weight of any rock that the octopus has hold of. The suckers of a large octopus are very strong: there is no way you can pull it off a rock. You are stuck. From that moment I tread carefully. It took two hours to fill our half bottles with *patalides* and I was pleased to get home. Georgos' mother enjoyed the *patalides*. I preferred the *ouzo*.

One method of catching fish on the island is to dive and shoot them with a spear gun. To do this you need a wetsuit, to keep you warm and stop the rocks, barnacles and sea urchins from shredding your skin and you need weights and a speargun. You also need to understand a little physics. The weights are there to counteract the buoyancy of the wetsuit and to enable you to descend with speed. As you dive the pressure of the water contracts your lungs and pushes you deeper; you dive down and swim up. Hunting with scuba equipment is forbidden so the depth we reach is limited by the length of time we can hold our breath. Diving with Georgos is a privilege: when he was young he shot fish at 30 metres. Even now he dives down to more than 25 and he doesn't just touch the bottom and return: he gets down to that depth and works: hunting this fish, shooting that, threading the fish onto the line, shooting another then up to the top again for a few deep breaths and down again. Each dive lasts more than a minute, and in the summer he dives for over six hours a day. Half the time he is under the sea. A friend of ours, a marine biologist, went diving with him one time. I asked what it was like and was told:

Until now I never saw a man swim better than a fish.

The first time I went diving with Georgos I was petrified; not for me, but for him. We anchored the boat south of Assilia, just past the beach of Papa Minas. Georgos outlined the plan as we put on our wetsuits and flippers and weights and inflated the red balloons that all divers must have to alert passing boats. For my safety we would keep within sight of one another and head down the coast in parallel, with me close to the shore while Georgos explored the rocks further out. Into the sea we went, splash, splash and with thumbs up started the hunt. Immediately I was upside down and entangled in my lines and by the time I was free Georgos had disappeared. Alone I headed south following a trail of fish scales and once, a cloud of ink that told me we would be eating octopus that night. I had yet to see a fish and still could not see Georgos. Then the water got deep and further out I saw him on the surface studying the rocks below. One harpoon gun hung from his balloon together with half a dozen fish. A larger gun was in his right hand, primed and ready to shoot. With his left hand he made strange movements curving his hand up and down and around. He was shaping the route he would take to the bottom of the sea; for what the hand describes the body follows. And then he was vertical in the water and heading down fast. From the surface he had seen, or he already knew, a hole under the rock 20 metres below, where there were likely to be fish. From the top I looked in horror as he reached the bottom and squeezed himself into the hole and, except for his blue, surprisingly long flippers, disappeared. Panic. Suppose he got stuck. What would I do? There is no way I could dive to that depth and now there were great silver bubbles from the top of the rock formation as he breathed out and was it imagination, or was the line attaching him to his balloon caught on a rock? How could I wait around while my friend died? I dived down to take a closer look, but when I got to my limit I was still 10 metres short. I hovered uncertainly for a few seconds before returning breathless and the wrong way up, to the surface. Trying to decide what to do next I saw Georgos appear backwards out of the hole with a large silver fish, *sargos*, on the end of his harpoon. He turned slowly and with a sudden blur of flippers shot to the surface. I waved and hoping I looked nonchalant and cool, continued on my way.

I saw several fish that day, but did not shoot any. They kept moving away. Georgos shot about 10 kilos. Not bad if you sell them, but not much if you have an extended family to feed. And me. For always, at the end of the day, before the last dive, Georgos will ask what fish I want that night and down he goes into the dark before bobbing up with that very fish on the harpoon and laughter in the air.

Since that first day we have dived many times together: some weeks we are out five or six days, for ten or more hours a day in, on, or under the sea. Now I too know where there are rocks with holes and where there are fish and what variety and how they behave. Ten metres is my limit, but that is enough to shoot my supper. We dive all over the north of the island and around Saria. I know the coast sufficiently well that I can lie in bed at night, thousands of kilometres away and retrace my way underwater, visit caves and dark canyons and see, once again, the fishes that got away. Georgos and I work like a twin-headed machine. I am the junior partner and my job is to get him to the right place in the right weather conditions and help him get into the water as fast as possible and stay there as long as possible.

Sometimes he shoots a big fish and needs help. I was in the boat one time going to pick him up. He had shot a 15 kilo *rokfos*, a grouper, in 20 metres of water. It had gone into an L-shaped cave and Georgos could not get it out. Fish like this are as strong as a large bulldog and their fins and gills are razor sharp. This one had jammed the harpoon between rocks and Georgos had to squeeze himself into the cave and then turn into an offshoot in order to seize the fish and wrestle it out; at 20 metres depth on one breath of air. My job was to stay on the surface and pass over various metal bars and nylon line while Georgos gradually extricated the fish. It took 5 hours to bring it slowly to the surface and, still alive, into the boat. Georgos was exhausted but carefully scaled and gutted the fish as we made our way back to the village in the dark. At my house he went into the kitchen mysteriously, and I heard the sound of a frying pan. Ten minutes later he appeared with the fish liver. As we ate he told me:

This is for the fishermens.

I was very proud.

My most important job, wherever I am at the end of the day, is to take the boat and collect Georgos. This is not as easy as it sounds, for the sea is big and there are currents and Georgos can cover several kilometres in an afternoon and worst of all we rendezvous at dusk. Descriptions like:

I will meet you by that big rock near the steep cliff, where you shot the *rokfos* two years ago

are open to misinterpretation, so I try to ensure we go through the arrangements in English as well as Greek. I have not lost him yet, though have come close a couple of times. Once we were diving north of the village. I left Georgos in his favourite spot and headed north to mine.

After five hours I was tired and had enough fish for my needs. I got back into the boat and sheltered out of the wind, under the cliffs at the cape.

The sun warmed and dried me as I waited for it to set in order to give Georgos maximum time in the sea. As it grew dark I headed south towards the rendezvous. But Georgos wasn't there. The light would last for another ten minutes, so I headed back to the cape and came slowly south again, peering into the dusk, hoping to catch sight of a red balloon. Nothing. I carried on further south. Still nothing. I passed the spot where I had dropped him. It was nearly dark and I was on the edge of panic. Nothing. Further south still? Wink, wink. Something gleamed among rocks close to the shore. I moved closer. By now it was dark and I was wary of the reefs. Wink. And then nothing.

Closer to the rocks and I could see the splash of a swimmer and the dark of a balloon and there he was. Georgos likes to shout when I make mistakes and I took my revenge. With much arm waving I stood in the boat and pretended I was angry, sprinkling my words with *malakas,* wanker, as well as *keretas* and much worse. Georgos said nothing. I maintained my outburst as he handed me the cord attached to the balloon. It was heavy as I pulled and into the boat came several silver fish, some sponges and an octopus. But there was something else. It was very heavy and came through the water with difficulty. Georgos swam around the fish delicately stroking its sides. It was a good fish and still alive. I leant forward and together we lifted the *synagrida* into the boat. We laughed and did high-fives and Georgos hoisted himself into the boat with one simple movement. A skill which even now I cannot emulate. He told me the story:

> Seven kilos, a good fish. It took hours to catch.
> Round and round it went, away and back again. With

a valuable fish like this you cannot take a risky shot. I was on his territory. He wanted to guard it. I waited and one time he came back and I got him. Seven kilos. I took so long the torch battery went flat. I signalled three times and then nothing.

So Georgos escaped a long swim home. Another time when I lost him was more serious. We were two hours away from the village, as I left him in a bay on the west side of the island, while I went to find calm seas. I found no fish worth shooting, but waited till dusk before returning to the rendezvous spot. He was not there. Only one thing is more lonely than being two hours away from home in a rough sea when the sun has gone down and that is being in that situation having lost your friend. I went out to sea to get a better view, stood up in the boat and peered around, but saw no hint of a red balloon. Wary of the rocks, I turned into the straits of Steno and slowly, slowly headed east. Waves pounded the rocks all around me and the wind whipped spray and foam horizontally, soaking me and leaving my glasses smeared with salt. How to see in these conditions and what to do if I can't find Georgos? Go to the village for help, go back and try to find him again? And then the signal far away in the dark. Wink. Wink. Wink. Thank God! And there he was on a rock like Poseidonas of old, sitting in the seaweed and the foam and holding up a harpoon with a good sized *kefalos*, grey mullet, that would be our supper. He tried to be angry with me, but knew he had moved far from the agreed spot and didn't even manage one *malakas*. On the way back I fished for *loutsos* while Georgos stretched across the oars and fell asleep.

How Georgos fell into the sea

Georgos started the day with good intentions. He had been fishing the night before, the sea was calm and he had anchored the boat on the mole. In the morning the wind changed and he wanted to move the boat to the shelter of the rocks. It was 8 am and he was a little sleepy. Maybe that is why he did not notice the sheen of oil on the concrete as he walked through the spilt diesel. He sat on the edge of the mole, paused a while then launched himself gently onto the prow of the little boat. And slipped.

Being an agile man he turned and took hold of the edge of the mole. Being a big man and unable to avoid the consequences of either Newton's laws, or that of gravity, a drama slowly unfolded. To start with the boat moved away from the mole. As a result Georgos' body lowered towards the horizontal and his grip on the concrete loosened. Approaching 45 degrees his position became untenable. He abandoned the boat and swung himself towards the mole. His feet got wet as did the bottom of his jeans. The extra weight of the water added to his problems. Gamely Georgos clung on to the mole and swung along towards the shore. After two metres his strength and resolve faded and he slowly subsided into the sea.

Nobody in the *cafeneion* saw this happen. They did see a commotion in the water and at first thought it to be a big fish or a Monk Seal. Wearing sunglasses, Raybans, Georgos swam to the shore, his mind frantically searching for an explanation. He reached the beach, stood up with water pouring from every pocket, nook and crevice and explained to the men in the *cafeneion*:

I saw a big octopus and dived.

Dinos looked at him. Weighed up the situation:

Where is the octopus?

It got away.

Georgos never loses an octopus. Dinos said so and told him:

I don't believe you.

and the *cafeneion* roared with laughter at Georgos' back as he trudged off, leaving a trail of running water and wet footprints.

And that's how Georgos fell into the sea.

The People of the Village

It is not easy writing about the people of the village. They are my friends, I like them, I cannot pretend to be dispassionate and, it must be said, I want to continue living among them. So I tread carefully: I try to be honest and clear and avoid unnecessary offence, yet strive to bring the subject alive.

I have known Minas Prearis for years. A little man, a few years older than me, he is Georgos' real and my surrogate father. He expresses love like no man I have ever known. When I go away he tells me he will worry about me until I return. When I return, he sits close to me in the *cafeneion* as I take my *ouzo*, sometimes holding my hand. Minas is a hypochondriac. Ask how he is and you receive a litany of ailments. His knee hurts, his blood sugar level is high, he cannot sleep and of course he no longer has sex:

> It is winter down there. The hands of my clock are
> stuck at half past six.

This might be considered a private matter, but I have heard his wife, Marina, shout out from her balcony when I asked where he was:

> Sleeping. Absolutely useless. He only sleeps.

Marina is a big lady, continually scolding her much abused husband. One time she arrived at Gabriella's with some fresh bread for me. Sitting down slowly and carefully, while muttering under her breath, she suddenly turned to me waving one hand just above the floor:

Have you seen how small he is?

As if she has only just noticed after 50 years of marriage.

But there is love and sometimes it is revealed. Minas was a great musician in his younger days, one of the best. Even now he reaches heights that others avoid. Twenty years ago he was awesome: a John Coltrane of the *lyra*, he improvised like no one had done before and took the music to the edge and beyond. His status is recognised: I entered a bar late one night in *to chorio*, the village up on the mountain. A small group of teenagers were gathered round an old cassette player listening to a tape. It was Minas and they were trying to understand how he played this note or extended that and how he had the audacity to do what he did and still keep the audience with him.

Now, when the young people play, it is possible to hear Minas' music shine through. Minas rarely plays these days, there is a macho element to playing at festivities: the musicians compete for money and play for hours on end. Occasionally a *lyra* or *lauto* player will take a break for a minute or two while they rub their hands in neat whisky to ease the pain in their fingers, but the music goes on: it is relentless. Minas tells me his fingers are not strong enough, he no longer has the stamina and while he will sometimes play for me or other friends I thought I would never hear him play in public again. But I had reckoned without Michaeli, also a well respected musician though, with his proclivity to play Cretan style *lyra*, considered to be slightly left field. Michaeli has a fine voice and an encyclopaedic knowledge of traditional songs. He is also *meraklis*, a musician who can orchestrate and conduct a *glendi*, festival, to cover the gamut of emotions. A year ago I stumbled into a village *glendi* a little late. Michaeli was playing *lauto* and, to my surprise, Minas was swinging away on the *lyra*. The trills were there, the swoops and flights of fantasy and ecstasy as, head back and far away, Minas peered beatifically upwards through his pebble-thick glasses. I sat next to my old friend, found a glass and lifted an *ouzo* to his throat and of course pushed his glasses back up his nose.

Later I was told the expected *lyra* player had not turned up and Michaeli had asked Minas to play:

Just for five minutes.

They had been playing for more than three hours when I arrived and were singing *mantinades*, the rhyming couplets that are integral to the festivals here. At first I could not follow the words, but slowly realised they were singing about Minas. Not about his hypochondria, his size, or his grumbles, but Minas the *meraklis*, who had been a great dancer, Minas the musician who showed us the way, Minas the lover with good looks and flashing smile, Minas, the village Romeo. All the while he sat there concentrating on the music, trilling away on the *lyra* as if they were singing about someone else. And then his son began to sing. The *mantinada* must have been formulating in Georgos' mind for some time, for these things are rarely instant compositions. He wanted to sing verses about his father which conveyed his love, respect and trepidation: verses which all of us should sing if we could, but one line just would not come out:

What shall we do when his music stops?

is a simple translation, but Georgos could not say the words. The lines stuck in his throat. Holding back tears strangled his voice and he could not finish the verse. Two or three times he tried and by now we knew what he wanted to say and we helped. Softly, at first, we sang along, gently giving support to his voice until finally Georgos gave full throat to his thoughts about his father and the chorus rang back:

What shall we do when his music stops?

and I could see that Minas was crying as was I and many others in the hall. Now we had our *glendi,* we had the catharsis of feelings shared with fellow men and women and we were glad. Minas played for another two hours until he could play no more. He handed his *lyra* to the next musician, shook hands with those around him, held me and kissed me, and left. The party went on until dawn.

In the morning the village knew something special had happened. There was an air of satisfaction, a feeling that something that should have been said long ago had finally been said. I was sitting in the Gorgona when Marina came past. She paused:

> I am so proud of him. So proud. That's what he was like when I married him. A great musician. A *meraklis.* Such a lover.

As if on cue Minas appeared. I told him:

> Last night you were great. *Maestoras.* A maestro. *Ti kaneis simera*? How are you today?

> Well my fingers hurt and there is a pain in my side and I am sure the sugar level has gone high.

Of course we laughed, but there was concern in our laughter, even from Marina. A few weeks later, in the evening after some drinks, a group of us were loudly discussing love and friendship. There was a pause for breath and from behind I heard a soft voice:

> *Pios ma agapai*? Who will love me?

It was Minas and with those words he opened a window and I could see inside. The village Romeo still wants to be loved.

Manos

Manos is a quiet man, *semnos*, a man of stature. Despite his good looks he is shy, not by nature, but by behaviour. Manos is offended by the cameras and the eyes of foreigners: he wants to be alone with his thoughts, away from intrusion. He wants to lead the old life and has lived alone so long that he feels better in his own company. Normally he can be found in a small house among terraces along the coast; he keeps chickens and goats, fishes from his little boat, looks after his olive trees and tends vegetables. Worried about his isolation a kindly neighbour gave him a cat for company and that was the beginning of his problems. At first he thought the cat was stand-offish or just did not like him. It was six weeks before he realised the cat was deaf. A strange present for a man living alone.

Occasionally Manos comes to the village. For a short visit this is simple: he launches his boat and chugs north along the coast and if the wind is in the right direction, he raises a small triangular sail; a romantic sight for the tourists who click away and dream of a better life. Longer visits cause problems. Goats and chickens cannot be left by themselves for long, they and their food have to come in the boat. A goat is an eating machine, it gives meat and milk and produces fertiliser for the fields but it must be fed. A man or woman can only carry enough goat fodder on their back for one goat for two days, or two goats for one day.

One time in the summer of last year, Manos planned to come to the village for three days. He had two goats so he spent several hours scything his meadow and it took three trips down to his boat, his back bent, legs straining, while he sweated under the itchy, green loads. Then up the hill again to fetch the goats gently down to the beach, cajole, lift and threaten them into the boat and tie them to the mast so they wouldn't escape while he fetched his chickens. And the deaf cat. Manos was tired when he set off in the hot mid-afternoon. The wind was soft and from the northeast so after a while he raised his sail and relaxed to the slap of the waves and the rush of the sea. Even the cat was at ease sitting in Manos' lap as he headed east to go outside the rocks that lurk off shore. Manos was at peace as he tacked northwest following the coast and rounded the cape heading towards the breakwater. At peace until he could get a clear view of the beach. Then he saw the *Chrissovalandou*, the tourist boat, still tied up at the mole and tourists scattered along the beach and he knew he would attract attention. No tourist could resist the photo opportunity of a man in a boat with chickens and goats.

Bringing a small boat into the village is not easy. There are rocks and large stones just off the beach and you have to chose the landing spot carefully. Doing this under sail is a tricky operation, but Manos achieved it smoothly and felt a sense of relief when the boat crunched ashore. He stood up to furl the sail. Unfortunately he forgot the cat. The cat fell into the sea. Manos leant over to scoop the cat out of the sea. The boat tilted. A chicken fell into the sea. Manos grabbed it. The other chickens flapped and squawked and took off from the boat. The goats startled by the commotion left the boat at speed and set off up the beach.

They were still tied to the mast. The boat is light and goats are strong. Two girls were sunbathing topless on the beach. This is offensive to the villagers, but they did not care. They were dozing as the chickens flapped overhead and were not fully awake as the goats, still attached to the boat, sped between them. They were, however, wide awake and suddenly alert as the boat ground to a halt and bundles of goat fodder fell on them. What they thought of the red faced Manos standing in the stern with a soaked cat in one hand and an irate chicken in the other is not recorded, but it is clear that they were not happy ladies. They screamed. The goats took off once again and Manos fell over backwards releasing both the chicken and the cat. Having goat food all over your tits is one thing, a wet cat and a disgruntled chicken quite another. The girls screamed again and the goats set off one more time. Mercifully the rope tying them to the boat snapped and they careered up the beach leaping over prone tourists like champion steeplechasers. The topless girls covered themselves up and ran to the sea to wash off the rustic debris and a crowd began to gather. Manos arose once again from behind the gunnels of his boat. He felt the concentrated gaze of the beach upon him and heard a hubbub of voices. He stepped out onto the pebbles, gathered a load of fodder and walked as slowly as was dignified to the sanctuary of the dark, narrow alley that leads to his house. The goats being, sensible creatures, were mainly interested in food and trotted quietly after him.

I saw all this happen, but when I tell the story Manos denies it and I doubt my memory. He does colour a little and admits that one time he owned a cat and it was deaf, so maybe it is a true story, and maybe Manos is his name.

Going to the Doctors

Going to the doctors in the west, is a private, secret, lonely affair. You catch a bus or drive alone, enter a waiting room, mumble quietly to the receptionist, try to keep your name confidential and take a seat as far as you can from the other patients. After a while you are called, you knock at a door and there is the doctor. Surrounded by stainless steel, enamel and machines you complete your business and you leave as discretely as possible. You may never see that doctor again, in street or surgery.

In the village it is different. To start with, everybody knows your name, and pretty soon they will know why you are here:

> *lati esai edw*? Why are you here? What's wrong with you?

And you have to explain. Be it haemorrhoid, verruca or cancer of the colon, they want to know. Even if at first you avoid explaining exactly what is the problem they will press until they know all the painful and gory details. They are not being rude or nosy. As fellow villagers they hope you will get better and they cannot wish you well if they don't know what is wrong with you. Then, there is the sharing of the gifts. It is normal in the village to take a small gift when you visit the doctor. Not to gain special advantage, but as a sign of respect for a learned profession. Nothing expensive: some lemons from your tree, artichokes perhaps, figs or something freshly baked. And because you are all together, perhaps five or six in a space with room for three or four you are soon chatting and sharing gifts. One patient is Anastasia, 88 years old and sprightly as a spring lamb. Her eyes are a bright, baby blue and she dances around as she asks how I am. Her hands are bent and crippled with arthritis, but she drags her goats here and there and carries their food up and down the steep mountainsides around the village and in Saria. Last night she was in my yard trailing two baby goats, looking for their mother. She tells me where she found the mother and laughs, but her dialect, without t's, d's, g's, or seemingly any recognisable consonant is difficult to follow. Then she reaches into the folds of her apron and hands me three lemons. She will be killing goats soon, she says, so if I need any kind of meat associated with a goat then she will find me some.

Another customer is my neighbour Calliopi. Her friend is with her, a woman known to me only as Thea (aunty). These are big women, very big women, they have trouble with diabetes exacerbated by lack of exercise. They live in little houses, side by side, at the bottom of the steps leading to my house. All day they sit on the steps in the shade, crocheting while they gossip. They remind me of the mythical black rocks, *tis sumplugades petres*, which used to crush ancient ships trying to sail between them. Only the Argonauts managed to pass through relatively unscathed. When these ladies are at the bottom of my steps I know that nobody will bother me. Calliopi gives me *koulouri*, the hard bread, round like a doughnut, that is so good in the summer when dampened with cold water, dipped in olive oil and eaten with olives or salty cheese. Meanwhile, Thea has been ferreting around in her apron and hands me fresh walnuts. They ask me why I am here, sympathise by saying it will get better and tell me a little of their ailments. I do not probe.

A widow and a 90 year old man, reputed to own half the village, arrive. I stand up to give them space and step outside to rest from the constant chatter. Everyone is talking to everyone else, sharing gifts and cursing old age and decrepitude. One by one we are called in to see the doctor.

The village does not do badly by the Greek medical service. Doctors in Greece have to work in a remote place before being given their full licence and being allowed to practice in Athens and on the mainland: so we have a series of young doctors on a six month, or one year placement. This works surprisingly well. There is mutual respect and the villagers are surprisingly tolerant to whoever is sent to us, be they gay or straight, man or woman. With the six port police that are stationed here, the occasional policeman and the young visiting schoolteachers, there is plenty of opportunity to form a *parea*, a company of friends. In the summer there are picnics and parties and the young doctors seem to like their stay. Every month a Flying Dolphin hydrofoil comes from Rhodes, with doctors, nurses and paramedics. Then a straggle of old people crank their way at different speeds to the end of the harbour, with their corns and coughs and pains and general complaints. The Flying Dolphin can do x-rays and blood tests and so provides the services of a travelling hospital. Serious problems have to be dealt with in the south of the island, or you take the ferry boat to Rhodes. But the real crunch is this: if you are taken suddenly ill and are not too old, then a helicopter will come to take you to Rhodes or Athens. If you are over 70 they tell you the weather is bad and to hang on a little longer. You can hang on as long as you like, but the weather will not clear if you are too old. So, no matter how many times I am asked, I never reveal my age and my passport is well hidden.

The Turks

Those of you who have met Kosmas know him to be a kind, gentle man, with no evil thoughts. Of course he is considered strange, but then he is sick and has been for many years. Schizophrenia is the layman's diagnosis, 'though there must be an element of autism as well. Schizophrenic people sometimes have a problem with sounds: they cannot differentiate between important sounds and background interference and this can make conversation difficult. Sometimes they hear voices. Many people hear voices, it is quite natural, we think of them as thoughts and keep them inside our heads. For others, the voices are separate from the self and this is difficult to admit.

One recommended approach for those who hear disembodied voices is to answer them and maintain a conversation. Mobile phones have made it easier to do this in public, as observers are unaware there is nobody on the other end of the phone. Kosmas is often distracted by voices and you can tell from his face that his mind has wandered off. Nicotine helps him concentrate as does alcohol. He enjoys his *ouzo*. Kosmas has a number of party pieces that amuse us. He likes to repeat the same things over and over again: his date of birth, the names of his four sisters and three brothers, *mantinades* written by his father, or stories he has told us before. I have several exercise books filled with Kosmas' handwritten letters composed with great care. They reflect his obsessions before he became ill and his memory cells were severely affected. Normally there is a request:

Mia fanellan Anglian. Podosforon. Liverpoon, **Rush**. *Enia.
Kokinon.*

An English football shirt. Liverpool. Rush (a footballer
from the 70's). Number nine. Red.

His party piece is to recite an imaginary football game
full of exciting details and names of half forgotten conti-
nental footballers; O Cruyft, Keiser, Rep, O Beckenbaur and
so on. Sometimes a crowd of young people will gather: half
a dozen or more bystanders shouting goal, or shoot or off-
side as Kosmas leads us deeper and deeper into a fantasy
game from long ago. Kosmas is genuinely loved by *to
chorio*. His mother died a while ago and he now lives in
Rhodes with his sister. He is well looked after and wanders
around the old town looking for people from the village
and tourists who have known him over the years. When I
met his sister for the first time she told me:

Ah, you are the Englishman he loves so much.

And I cried.

Sometimes Kosmas comes back home to the village.
Then I sit with him in the evening, in some bar or other,
much to the confusion of the visitors, who see a strange
and scruffy Greek writing letters and *mantinades* while he
talks to himself and a strange and scruffy Englishman.
Kosmas is an innocent man who exudes peace and warmth.
Like a favourite cat, he makes you feel at home.

Georgos, Kosmas, myself and Nikos Karellas tend to
form a *parea*: the four *mousquatiars*, though I will not iden-
tify D'Artagnan. Karellas has a pony tail, bent nose and
missing teeth, at least one of which is my responsibility and
looks like an Apache straight off the reservation in a 1940s
western. Sometimes the four of us get into trouble. One
time I was out of the village, but Georgos and Karellas
wanted to go to Tristomo. It was a nice day and there was a

panegyri, festival, in the little church of the Archangel
Michalis: there would be dancing, drinking, good food and
an overnight stay. Kosmas was apprehensive but, with the
promise of an evening's alcohol, agreed to go. So, three
mousquatiers took my boat and set off in a calm sea. Tristomo is an hour or more away and they arrived just as the
music was starting. There are no beds at this kind of gathering. The guests are hardy people: they eat, drink, sing and
dance and when they are totally exhausted they lie down
on the ground and sleep. In the morning Karellas and
Georgos awoke late. They looked around, everything
seemed fine, but Kosmas was missing. They asked and were
told he had set off early in the morning to walk back to the
village. There are footpaths to Tristomo, but Kosmas does
not know them. He went in roughly the right direction, but
straight up the barren mountain. All for one and one for
all: Georgos and Karellas decided to go back to the village
to make certain that Kosmas was safe. There was a stiff
breeze but these two are experienced boatmen and there
would be no problem. The waves were two metres high as
they left the lagoon of Tristomo, so to avoid getting wet
they headed northwest into the wind and away from the
rocks. Soon they were sufficiently far out to turn east and,
with the wind behind them, head through the straits of
Steno.

There is always a strong current in Steno, though it
changes direction twice a day. Now it was behind them and
they sped along trawling for barracuda and looking for
lathiro, flotsam. This feels like going to a jumble or car boot
sale, but instead of a bargain, the primitive instinct of the
hunter-gatherer takes over in the search for something for
nothing. They were lucky. They found something exciting:
a three metre pole floating along in the sea. Shortly after,
there was something else, something inexplicable: a flag:
Turkish. Unabashed the two *mousquatiers* raised the flag on

their newly acquired pole and continued on their voyage. Soon they turned south to Alona, where strong winds came from every direction. They passed Amoi, Troulakas and Mavri Petra and by the time they were at the cape they were in sight of the village. Until now there had been no glimpse of Kosmas.

Kalamnia is a favourite beach of mine: backed by steep cliffs it has cool caves and it is considered inaccessible by foot. At the north end of the beach there are submerged rocks where barracuda gather. As the voyagers headed towards this spot Karellas saw a figure on the beach. It was Kosmas, waving and shouting. How he got there is still a mystery, but there he was, running up and down:

Boethia, boethia. Help me, help me.

Shouting his name they came closer. Kosmas saw two men in a boat, heard them shout and ....saw the Turkish flag. He paused for a second, then with all the instinct of a Greek brought up on stories of Turkish atrocities during the Greeco-Turkish wars, turned and ran away. Georgos is not built for speed: slow downhill being his favourite gear, but he leapt out of the boat with agility and ran after Kosmas. By now the poor man had started climbing up the cliff:

Boethia, boethia. Tourkos, Tourkos.

Followed by Georgos shouting:

Kosmas. Kosmas.

Before collapsing on the beach, giggling and out of breath. Kosmas hid behind a large rock. Georgos shouted for him to come out:

No.

Why not?

Eisai Tourkos.

I am not a Turk. I am Georgos.

Georgos? *Sto dialo*? What the devil? Are you Turkish now?

No.

Are you sure?

Certain.

Do you have any water?

Yes.

Ekeis cigara? Do you have a cigarette?

Yes.

So they were together again. One of them confused, but safe. The others laughing and giggling. I have tried to imagine this drama with other characters. I cannot. It could only happen to these three *mousquatiers*.

Death in the Village

He was killed by his boat: a heavy boat, an old boat, *maiounas*, built of pine a hundred years ago in Turkey or Symi. Or maybe it was the engine that killed him: the faltering, stuttering, feeble engine that failed in the wrong place at the wrong time: four kilometres from home in a strong southwest wind. Or perhaps the anchor that would not hold and forced him and his old wife to row too far, for too long. We knew there was a problem, all the boats were pulled up on the beach out of the reach of the waves, all except for one. A *caique* set out to help and found them battling the seas under the cape. They threw a rope and were towed back to the village and safety. But of course he was an independent man and close to home, he took the oars again and rowed to the beach. We laid *fallangi,* the long planks of wood over which we slide boats; we took the boat and pulled it up out of the water and helped the old man and his wife onto the stones. He was a proud man, but clearly in pain, as he went back to his boat to tidy away the oars and he laid down and died of a heart attack.

In the village we bury the dead as soon as we can. His son came from Athens the next morning and his daughters too. The women of the village were at the dead man's house: they prepared the body, sat the night with him, comforted the family and sang laments. *To chorio* echoed with their wailing. The time of the funeral was fixed to occur when the last tourist bus had left and we gathered and we waited. Waiting for a funeral is not like waiting for a bus: there are no light moments to alleviate the boredom:

you just wait: you look bad, you feel bad and you wait. A car from the south was delayed by rain and we waited for two unbearable hours. Suddenly the relief of a bell:

Ding, ding. Ding, ding. Ding, ding.

and a small, sad, procession leaves the home of the dead man to find its way through the narrow streets to the church.

Ding, ding. Ding, ding. Ding, ding.

First the coffin lid carried by Iannis, then a collection of heavy brass crosses, centuries old and dull with patina, then the open coffin held aloft by six strong men. As it comes close I hear the cry of the daughters:

Pateras mou. Pateras mou.

then see the wife: silent, with her shawl pulled down and her long grey hair swirling in the wind. There are women on either side to carry her if she falls. They push into the church. It is full inside and there is not room for all of us, so we wait in the cold. The whole village is here, maybe four hundred people, for the dead man was a good man and this death is tragic. The men are dressed in an assortment of clothes, some formal, some not. But it is the women in the *kavai*, the ancient black shawl and long dress and apron and proud, handmade boots: it is the women who look in place, for this is an old village and these are ancient people:

Ding, ding. Ding, ding. Ding, ding.

The procession comes out of the church into the pale autumn light: the coffin, the brass crosses and then the family and the close friends and the rest of us. We thread through the lanes and alleyways, tripping and stumbling on the time-worn steps. There is the sound of soft shoes, the squeak of boots, sobs and coughs and snuffles. In a crush of people I try not to touch or be touched, I try to remain apart. Slowly we move down to the cemetery as wails and jeremiads mix with the wind and the women rend their clothes and scratch their faces and pull their long grey hair and keen and cry.

In the cemetery there is chaos. It is too small for so many people and everyone wants to get close to the coffin, to be near that poor, poor man. They press forward and strong men push them back and there are struggles and shouts. The cemetery is far from the village and the graves are not visited every day, so relatives of the recently deceased gather round the tombs and cry for their mother, or maybe a child and their moans are taken to the clouds. People look left and right to see who they can comfort: for this is what the village is for: this is collective grief. Then the sharp sound of a spade as it cuts the soil and the dull thud of rocks on wood and the coffin is covered and a good man is gone. Now the children scream and my heart is torn by the question:

Pateras mou. Pou tha pame tora? My father. Where do we go now?

There is no answer. There can be no answer. I see friends holding the son, I see the distraught daughters lying on the ground, I see grim faces and I turn and walk up the path. I see fellow fishermen gathered together in a group. We avoid one another's eyes. It could happen to us, but we say nothing, only:

Take care. Take care.

Someone quotes a *mantinada*. A rough translation:

Do not ask for whom the bell tolls. Tomorrow it is for you.

Exhausted, I leave the cemetery. I am glad to be gone. The call of a raven breaks the silence and then, suddenly, I am alone.

Requiem

The only formal Greek classes I went to were in North Wales. The teacher was Margo, a fierce lady with a fine sense of humour. Short and dumpy with black curly hair, she smoked compulsively and loved her students. Margo never had any money, but there was always a head blowing Greek coffee for us and sometimes biscuits or homemade cakes. We were mature students of different backgrounds and abilities, but we worked together and did our best for our teacher. Once a week we squashed into her council flat to be scolded for mistakes we made, or homework not done. I was living alone in a wild and remote place at the time and drove through flood and storm, snow, wind and hail to reach these Wednesday night classes: the highlight of my week.

Margo's story encapsulated much that is Greece, but we had to wheedle it from her. People in Britain felt they were hard done by following the Second World War, but their suffering was as nothing compared to other parts of Europe. During the Greek civil war (1945-1949) Margo and her older sister were kidnapped and taken away from home by communists. This tactic was used by both sides, the intention being to raise children in the captor's ideology; hundreds of thousands were held in this fashion. Margo was around six years old, her sister was eight and very smart. Conditions were bad and soon the two girls were bitten by fleas. The sisters deliberately scratched the bites till they grew red and filled with puss, then they faked a fever and told the captors they had smallpox. They were expelled from the camp and hand in hand walked across a hostile and shattered landscape for two weeks: begging and stealing food on the way, sleeping in barns and sheepfolds. Miraculously the children found their way home, but the family travails were not over: Margo's brother died of starvation.

Margo grew up a hard-working and independent woman, she eventually met Lazarus, a lovely man, who for reasons I cannot explain came to live in North Wales and raise goats. Margo joined him and the pair opened up a small sweetshop in the damp and inward looking village of Llangernw. The villagers refused to speak English to Margo so she learnt Welsh. Later she learned English and then French and Italian and the couple's son, Nick was brought up tri-lingual; English, Greek and Welsh. Margo was devastated when Lazarus died. She visited his grave regularly and teased us by saying that she would light two cigarettes and press one into the earth for him while she told him her news.

I left Wales to spend more time in Greece, but I kept in touch with Margo and my classmates. We exchanged Christmas cards and occasionally I visited Margo and Nick in their little house in Mochdre. Then came the call I had been expecting for some time. Margo had cancer, was very ill and had only a short time to live. A few days later Georgos and I went diving off Saria. I dropped him on the south coast and chugged slowly around to a little bay at the foot of *Agios Pantelemonos*, the church perched on a mountain top of the southwest corner of the island. The sea was calm, but there were few fish and for some reason I had no *kefi*, joy, for this work. After two hours I came out of the water, peeled off my wet suit, dried and got dressed. I walked up the steep path to the church, taking my time in the hot afternoon sun. Partridges made their protests in the surrounding scrub and the black shapes of Eleanora's falcons scythed the air.

The church was cool and dark. I am not a Christian, but for some reason was compelled to light a candle 'though I had no idea who it was for. I spent time outside the church, sitting in the shade, looking over the Aegean, concentrating on the islands of Astakida on the western horizon. Slowly I returned to the boat and edged along the coast to pick up Georgos. He had plenty of fish, and laughed when I told him I had none, but he picked up my sombre mood and we were quiet for much of the journey home. We chose our fish for the night and they were scaled and gutted by the time we arrived in the village. When I got home there was a text on my mobile. It simply said:

Margo died today.

I phoned Nick, who was sad, but coping. Knowing I could not make it back to the UK for the funeral Nick asked me:

Light a candle for my mum.

I have.

I told him:

I already have.

Going to Argos

Today there is going to be a *panegyri*, a festival for the name day of the church of Zacharia at Argos, high up above Palatia in the north of Saria. I want to go, but am frightened. Not of the reception I will receive, for sure I will be welcome, but of the weather. It is windy, the sea is rough and Palatia is a long way to travel in a small boat. I go to Gabriella's for a coffee, sit and look at the sea, think what it will be like in the north and grumble about the price of the coffee. Undecided, I walk back to my house. Slowly. On the beach I see Manolis and his son and grandson. They are loading up their boat. I see a lute being wrapped in a towel, a *lyra*, a bow, sleeping bags. They are going:

Pou pas. Where are you going?

Argos, to the festival.

Seeking comfort I ask:

Have you seen the weather?

Yes it's rough but what can we do. *Pas gialo gialo* and you will be alright.

Suddenly I am angry. Who are they to tell me to keep *gialo gialo*, close to the shore? What do they expect me to do in this weather? I have done the trip many times, I am hesitant, that's all. Aren't I? Half an hour later, I find myself casting off my boat from the rocks. I have my binoculars, a sweater, two bottles of water and a mobile phone for security. Of course the phone only picks up signals intermittently, but if I drift out to sea I might come across a spot where it works, before the boat fills with water.

The first ten minutes are easy. It is windy, but the cliffs protect me as I jink my way between the rocks. At Vananda the wind comes roaring down the valley and cold, wet spray stings my face as I turn too slowly into the wind. Minutes later, I turn back again, the wind becomes *prima*, from behind, and I can clean my spectacles. I pass Kalamnia and Kamarouka and round the cape. As expected the wind is strong and the waves begin. My little boat heaves and slaps the sea and the spray blinds me, but I keep well in and am under control. Mavri Petra, the Black Rock, comes and then Troulakas, black and ugly, as the *mantinada* goes and then it is rough, very rough. The wind accelerates down the mountainside, takes hold of my boat and tries to spin it away from the cliffs, but I need to be there *gialo gialo*: I need to be as close to the cliffs as possible. The open sea means death for me and for the boat. The waves are not a metre high, but they come at me with speed and the wind whips the tops into a white fury. I can see nothing, but use my face to feel the direction of the wind as I struggle to keep the safest course.

At Alona I need both hands on the tiller to keep heading into the wind and up goes the prow as the boat tilts and smashes down again, and the oars and the nets and all the fishing paraphernalia jig around. Empty water bottles fly about and I am forced to put my spectacles down on the anchor chain, so they are not blown off my face. I am scared, but cannot turn back; it would be suicide to go side on to this sea. On I plough: smash, whoosh, bang: spray, sunlight, sea, salt: water on my hair, water on my face, water running down my back. I am soaked. Fear has made me thirsty, but I need two hands on the tiller and cannot take a drink. I aim for the flat stretch of water that is always found just off the cape in this weather. Suddenly I am there, the sea is calm and I can relax.

I take off my shirt, wring it out and thread an oar through it so it will not blow away. I wash my spectacles, take a swig of water, bale the boat, stand precariously to take a pee and plan the next move. Steno is straight in front, the wind is from the west, the waves are bigger, but I know the trick. Tuck in behind this big rock, go into the wind, move out a little to get behind that rock, keep into the wind, then the little rock and we are dancing now as the wind takes me where it wants and slowly, slowly, slowly I turn and the wind is *prima* and I am safe. I have made it to Saria. I am halfway. And exhausted.

The west wind, passes through the narrow straits of Steno, then curls round the coast north and south. I head north and the wind is behind me and the current too. I have to pay attention to the waves. I have to go faster than the waves or they will break over the stern and into the boat and cause me problems. I do not need problems and am on edge for another half hour. I pass Sta Mairia and Asproas and then, without warning, the wind dies, the sea is calm and suddenly there is Palatia. I have survived. This time I have survived and I am grateful.

On the beach I see Manolis in his vest: his shirt hanging in a tree. He is pacing about while drying the lute case and cursing the weather, the sea, his son and for all I know, me. I laugh:

Vregmenos o coulo sou? Is your ass wet?

He asks and he laughs too: a deep, big bellied, mature man laugh that signifies hard times and shared dangers. We wait for our clothes to dry, tell one another we were not frightened and then we set off. Argos is at the top of the cliff. We are going to climb a mountain.

Argos

Argos is a deserted village high up on the cliffs in the north of Saria. I have been to the *panegyri* before. It is my favourite festival, organised by the families I am closest to, but this time it is different: I am lucky, I see the deserted village through another persons eyes. It is Manolis' first visit to Argos for half a century. He points to the *sterna*, an elegant semicircular stone construction built into the ground, just inland from the beach of Palatia. I see beauty in decay, Manolis sees possibilities for renewal:

> This once held water for the animals and could again: just dig out some stones here, excavate there and water will come; that would be good for the goats and good for the bees.

The path to the mountaintop follows a canyon formed by earthquakes and rain. It is steep. From time to time we stop to gain breath and once to let a young boy with two donkeys pass down to the beach to fetch provisions from the anchored boats. The path is badly degraded at one spot and Manolis tells me the name, *Kako Scala*, Bad Steps, and I think of villagers working together: fixing the steps; renewing the path: joking, gossiping, sweating in the sun. We are tired when we reach the top, but we pause longer than necessary.

On my previous visits I had seen broken walls and decayed houses. Manolis sees them too, but something else: he sees his own past, he sees his youth. His family has houses and land in Argos and when he left school at fourteen years of age he lived here with his sister for over a year. That was 1956: Elvis Presley was in the charts for the first time, there were H-bomb tests and the Suez crisis, while Khrushchev attacked the cult of personality surrounding Stalin. Manolis knew nothing of these things, only how to milk goats, catch fish, keep bees and survive without electricity and running water. Some of his friends never went to school, some did not even have their birth registered; the state still does not know they exist:

In those days there were more people living here than in Diafani. All the little *korafia,* terraces, were planted: they grew wheat, rye and barley. All the walls were maintained: that field was where we kept goats, this gap, full of rocks, was a road. We had figs, almond trees, *horta,* greens. Men would come from Diafani to tell us when to sow and when to reap. Every Saturday night there was a party and people would come from Diafani in their wooden boats. They would row for two or three hours, sing and dance all night and row back the next day. In the summer the wind would be against them on the way out, in the winter it would be with them and the journey back in the morning would be hard. The first outboard motor in Diafani was only 2.5 horse power. The owner would come up to Argos with his wife. When the wind was against him he would hand over the tiller to his wife and take the oars to help the engine. Sometimes a boat with four men rowing would be faster than him with his wife, his engine and his oars.

As Manolis speaks he brings the village alive: I hear children's voices, follow their songs, see them play; I see flocks of goats and sheep, hear the women call the children home to supper, a wooden spoon beat on a cooking pot. Manolis has taken us back half a century, but he is sad: in those days every family had a cow, there were donkeys, mules, sheep and goats. Now there is nothing.

We enter the village, take sweet water from a well and drink deep. It is dusk and more people are arriving. *Sariatis*, people of Saria, cross the wild, stony, mountain panorama. Maria Karellas has been been here all day, cooking over two wood fires: a big pot with goat, frying pans for meat balls, potatoes and onions. Oil lamps light the little houses: small stars in a dark village. There are more than fifty of us now: sitting, talking, greeting one another as if we had not met for generations. Manolis' brother Vassilis arrives with Nikos Karellas. He is wet and very angry: The sea was terrible he tells me. Ridiculous. Normally it is me who gets wet and I cannot hide my pleasure at his discomfort. I laugh. He looks at me with a hard, hard, frightening stare. There is steel, then he too laughs and I can relax again.

On the horizon, a hundred metres to the north, the silhouette of a wooden cross stands against a lowering sky. The church bell rings across the dry, scarred landscape and slowly we are drawn to the sound: stumbling in the dusk as we follow goat tracks and foot paths. Papa Minas is inside the tiny church chanting hymns and prayers and we stand outside huddled together against the wind. Soon the *papas* comes out of the church and blesses us and blesses the holy bread. We drink *ouzo*, offer greetings, take a piece of holy bread each and cross the stony fields once again.

It is dark now and Argos is lit up. A generator, hauled by donkeys up the mountain path, gives electricity and there are tables and chairs and goat stew and salad and *ouzo* and *retsina*. Papa Minas blesses the food and the assembly and we eat and drink. Then, as always, there is music. First there are Byzantine hymns, then songs of the islands, epics, ballads, love songs and finally *mantinades*. There is a scuffling in the dark and Konstantis appears, his hands full of dripping honeycomb. Then there is whisky and I knew it is time to go. On the roof of a goat house, in a dark corner, someone has laid down a sheep's wool mattress for me. I am given a pillow and blankets and crisp, clean, cotton sheets. Under the stars the sky is clear and I can see moons around Saturn. I hold the taste of whisky and honey and smell woodsmoke and goat shit as the rhythm of the *lauto*, the trill of the *lyra* and the voices of the men lure me asleep. And then it is morning.

Harri

You know that you belong to a village when you know the name of the dogs. Long ago there was Foula, who lived at Vananda and was later buried there, with full honours, including hymns and a coffin covered in the Greek flag. Then there was Menelaus who belonged to Gabriella. This harmless and not very bright little dog, was named after the brother of Agamemnon, the ruler of Sparta, whose wife ran off with Paris and was fetched back from Troy after a long and famous siege. Following old age and senility, Menelaus, the dog, was banished from the Gorgona restaurant and lived his last years in tranquillity in Italy. And of course, following the classical trend, there was Hector who was poisoned in mysterious circumstances and died in his owner's arms.

Of all the dogs from the village my favourite is Harri. He has a cheeky face and an eager tail but for reasons of propriety I have had to change his name. If you come to the village you will recognise him as the only dog ever to be allowed in to Anna's *cafeneion*. Well, not exactly inside, but onto the terrace: in the day-time that is. His owner is Nikos Karellas, an unlikely partner. The unique and mainly unknown aspect of Harri is that he is a shoe fetishist. You might find this surprising. There follows a story.

Georgos sleeps with his shoes outside his house. There is no particular reason for this but he doesn't wear shoes very often and they are always left outside. One day, one of his shoes disappeared. After many hours search he found it on the beach at the far end of the village: there were teeth marks and the lace had gone. Two days later, one of his wife's shoes went missing. By then he had marked Harri as a likely culprit and went up to Karellas' house to ask if they had seen a lady's shoe. They searched a dustbin and there it was: destroyed, with the same same teeth marks. Georgos was angry:

You owe me a pair of shoes.

Two weeks later and knowing nothing of these events, I was off to Rhodes to do some shopping. The ferry boat was due and I was walking with my little bag along the harbour. Among the crowd of fellow travellers, I noticed Georgos in shorts and *sayonaras*, flip flops, with a plastic carrier bag in each hand. He had a tooth ache, he explained and needed a dentist, the dentist was in Rhodes:

What's in the bag?

Fish.

Why?

To pay the dentist.

What's in the other bag?

Fish.

???

For the ticket.

At the time, Karellas was living in Rhodes and fixing up a rather battered Turkish *gulet*. Boats this size in Rhodes have their own harbour. We went there to sleep on the *gulet*. On arrival, we found it was rather scruffy compared to its neighbours, particularly the one next door: a private yacht of the Russian oligarch, Roman Abramovich. This towered above Karellas as he scrapped, hammered and painted away on the deck of the *gulet*. I am a Chelsea fan and was pleased to be sleeping near to our owner. In the early evening we sat on the aft deck and opened the first beers of the day. Like a homing pigeon, our friend Kosmas appeared out of the gloom. He was dressed in elegant, but threadbare clothes, with a pair of sunglasses, playboy style, perched on top of his head. It was like the old times: the four Musketeers together again. As the empties mounted up Harri wandered around the harbour at will, occasionally earning a pat on the head from the security guards around the bigger yachts. Suddenly he was back with something in his mouth: a man's sandal: leather, size 43, left foot, Gucci. We laughed:

   Theloume zefgari. We need a pair.

I told the little dog and he trotted off once again along the harbour. Ten minutes later has was back with something else: a man's sandal: leather, size 43, right foot, Gucci. We had a pair! 43 is Georgo's shoe size. The sandals were a perfect fit:

   There are your shoes,

Karellas told Georgos. We clinked cans. Harri wagged his tail. The security guards looked on suspiciously.

To be a Fisherman

Imagine you have the life of a Greek fisherman: freedom to roam the seas, go where you will, work when you want while you become tanned and fit in the sunshine. Wonderful. Think again. Think of a 10 metre boat: a cramped cabin, two or three men. Think of fishing in all weathers for 24 hours a day. In the evening you lay the nets or *paragadi* or *petonia*: in the morning you pick them up, you pull in the line or the net or the floats. The work has cut your hands deeply, they hurt, you are wet and the boat does not keep still. From the land the blue waves and white spray look pretty. From the land you do not notice if the wind is six, or seven, or eight Beaufort. From the land the sea does not look dangerous, and it is not, unless you are standing on wet nets and it is four in the morning, there is a blow and you have not slept for a day or two.

There are no bunks on the boat: you sleep on the nets: soft and damp, but relief for an hour or two. If you are lucky there is a litre of fresh water to wash your face and tip over your head when you wake, if not, it is the sea and the risk of salt water sores. There is no toilet. For comfort you shit on the rocks, at sea you shit in the sea, but only in daylight when the other men are awake to keep an eye on you. Alone you shit in a bucket and you throw the shit downwind or you buy the *ouzos* next time you are on land. You cannot swim. To learn to swim would be to tempt the fates and in any case, you wear long boots and you know they fill with water so fast they will drag you down. There is no point in learning to swim.

You live like this for six months a year: day in, day out, hour after hour. The captain is your brother, your father, your cousin; he may love you, but he cannot be your friend. One share of the profit goes to the owner of the boat, one share to the owner of the nets. Two shares to the captain. If there is one captain and two crew and the nets are not yours, you get one sixth. With luck and skill and hard work, the boat can catch 30 or 40 kilo of fish a day. That is an income, not profit, of 400 euros a day. For you 60 euros a day. For half a year. For this you work 18 or 20 hours every 24. You are scared, wet, tired, bored. You are disgusted with the conditions, you deprive your wife of a husband and your children of a father and you know, deep, deep down, you know you are destroying the sea: for each year there are fewer fish and the fish are smaller and each year your nets fill with more and more plastic. Of course you appear in photographs and videos taken by foreigners seeking the authentic Greece, but you do not love the life; you do this work for your children and because you have no choice. I asked a friend if he liked the life of a fisherman. He was emphatic:

> I want to live in a small house with a balcony and eat *souvlaki* all day.

He no longer fishes. In the summer he scrubs the decks and toilets on the tourist boat.

Fishermen tend to keep themselves to themselves, but they can be surprisingly erudite. One evening, I was in a bar, discussing the meaning of life and sharing *barbouni* and *raki* with fishermen from Kalimnos. We had drunk a lot and I was talking to the captain about his life. Knowing me to be a bit of a writer, he gave me a gift. He gave me poetry. His hands were cut and scarred by nylon, broken coral, fish bones and cruel hooks. He held them out for me to see:

Nobody should have hands like this. Nobody.

He did not need to expand and he said nothing about the danger or the difficulties. He didn't have to: they are etched on his hands and on his face. Fishing is one of the most dangerous occupations, but mishaps are rarely reported. What follows is from the In Karpathos web site, November 18th 2008:

> Today an Egyptian drowned in Saria. From first reports, he was working on a fishing boat and at around 5am, they told him to do something, but he was nowhere to be seen. Fishermen in Diafani were contacted for help. They went north to join in the search and found a body floating in the sea. They recognised him as an Egyptian. They think he was having a shit and fell into the sea. The body was brought to Pigadia. A witness at the harbour stated that there was blood coming out of his ears and mouth. Nobody knew his name.

The Urn

It is the little things that count, the small, hard to notice objects and activities that tell stories and lead you down paths you never planned to travel. For nearly thirty years I have been going to the same *cafeneion*, sitting in the same place, watching the same gestures, listening to the same conversations. Always the outsider, I sit and listen and try to learn. I do not want to intrude on the local people, the old men: for this is their sanctuary, their home, sometimes their parliament. Near where I sit, outside the *avli*, there is a white stone object, about 50 cm high, with a flagstone lid. I used to believe it came from some church or other, perhaps an ancient font. Maybe it did, but it has a more recent use, less exalted, more prosaic which illuminates recent village history and makes this little *cafeneion* a little more exotic:

Gourna.

Anna tells me. With her arms flailing around, her face alive:

Gourna, yia kompaneizei cafe. An urn to grind coffee.

And I am confused: her dialect is too strong and she speaks too fast. Trying to make me understand she shouts louder and waves her arms with more vigour:

Gourna, yia kompaneizei cafe. An urn to grind coffee.

Suddenly I do understand and the old village is reborn as Anna carries me back 50 years or more, to the time before the road was built, before electricity, before television and packaged goods and tourists. Anna has an audience now, as the old men turn to listen and she tells me she and her mother used to pound away at coffee beans in the urn and I understand another meaning of *cafeneion*. From the 19th century, in the days of sail, coffee beans came in bulk from Brazil to Piraeus and were then broken down into smaller packages for local transportation throughout Greece. In Anna's time beans came in sacks from a *caique*, maybe the Sebasti, that delivered general goods and groceries from Rhodes and unloaded them onto the mole across the road. Anna and her mother carried the sacks of coffee beans and stored them in the *apothekie*, cellar, under the bar, or perhaps on the *pano sofa*, the high platform you see, as you sit inside on chilly winters evenings. Other goods came too: *ouzo* and whiskey, tobacco and Turkish delight and sweets for the winners of card games. It was Anna's job to roast the beans. She would light the family oven, the old stone one by the beach, heat it to the right temperature and dry the beans in the oven. And then, she tells me, with agreement from the old men:

> The whole village smelt of coffee. *Pantou*. Everywhere.

And we are in a time of isolation, hardship and poverty, peace and rumour, superstition and storytellers and good music: a time when the *cafeneion* was, with the church, a twin centre of village life. Anna laughs, as she agrees with me that to fill the village with the smell of coffee was very, very smart marketing. When the beans were roasted they were placed in the urn and pounded for hour after hour by Irene, Anna's mother and by Anna herself. The pestle they used was the drive shaft of a marine engine a heavy object now hidden away in Olymbos awaiting the foundation of a village museum. The work was exhausting, she tells me, her arms ached for days.

Anna has little opportunity to express herself and looks pleased as she goes back to her embroidery. It is warm outside as I sit with my *ouzo* and look at the sea and dream a little. I feel the wind, hear the slap and swish of the sea and perhaps, the clip-clop of the feet of mules. I see a village lit by oil lamps and candles. It is quiet now except for the shouts of men but I cannot understand the words. Are they Greek or Italian or perhaps even Turkish? There is a delicious smell in the air. I have drunk enough.

Souvlaki

I never knew Captain Manolis. I saw him around the village, said hello a few times, but we were not friends. He was a good man: people speak highly of him and tell many stories: most of them funny. He was the captain of a sleek *caique*, a good captain but, like most of us, he made mistakes. One time, in a dead calm sea up by the cape, he hit a rock. Now this takes some doing. I hit the same rock myself once, but it was very windy, someone was blocking my view and I was new to the game. Captain Manolis had been plying the same way for nearly fifty years when he hit this particular rock. When his wife shouted at him, his excuse was:

It wasn't there last week.

Which still causes laughter among the old men at the *cafeneion*.

Another time, he set off from the village and then went below deck to fiddle with the engine. Unfortunately he had not noticed the little fishing *barca* 100 metres in front of him. Iannis Karellas was pulling in his *paragadi*, a long line used to catch the finest fish. He heard the *caique*, looked up and saw it bearing down on him, stood up and shouted, then screamed and at the last moment dived into the sea. Bang. There was a crash and lines, nets, oars and fishing paraphernalia were thrown out of the boat. The collision brought Captain Manolis back on deck. He looked around at the chaos, saw Iannis frantically paddling in the sea and casually asked:

What are you doing down there?

And Iannis, normally the mildest of men, told him.

A week or two later the pair were sitting in the *cafeneion* with the rest of the men. Captain Manolis stood up:

Paw psarema. I am off fishing.

Smiling gently, Iannis asked:

Which way are you going?

I go south. Why do you ask?

Iannis paused for a while:

I'll go north.

And the *cafeneion* fell about laughing as the captain looked around in bemusement.

Perhaps the most spectacular story concerns Souvlaki, a speedboat: the first of its kind to be seen in the village. Capable of 40 kph it was a beast of a boat and its owner, a distinguished Athenian, had great fun roaring round and round the little bay in front of the village making waves and foam and a lot of noise. Of course the old captain wanted to try and soon he was sitting in the cockpit being shown the controls. It was simple for an old hand like him and soon he was making his mark: banging the boat against the waves, bouncing up and down, doing seawater wheelies.

Twenty minutes passed and he turned back to the village. Planning to tie up against the mole he headed towards the *cafeneion* at high speed. Keeping one hand on the wheel he reached for the lever to slow his progress. It wasn't where he thought it was. He felt, he looked, he cursed, but couldn't find the lever. Too late to change direction, he headed towards the beach at top speed. In those days there was no road separating the *cafeneion* from the beach, just a gentle slope of sand and stones. Both hands on the wheel, head down, Manolis held on as Souvlaki hit the stones with a loud bang and with propeller screaming, slid the boat up the slope towards the *cafeneion*. Some of the younger men leapt out of the way. The older ones stood up. One, very old man, noticed nothing untoward. With a horrible scraping sound the boat gently came to a stop one metre from the nearest chair. Nobody was hurt, but they were frightened and in Greek fashion expressed their opinions:

Why the **** did you do that?

The reply added to the reputation of Captain Manolis:

I needed a coffee.

Reading the Signs

The wonders of Greek marketing continue. There is a new sign at the Gorgona restaurant:

GREAT ATMOSPERE

it announces. Gabriella's mistake is noticed with glee and she replaces it with last years announcement.

INTERESTING PEOPLE INSIDE

Unfortunately this gives umbrage to Papa Minas who, with Aristotelian logic, asks:

What does that say about those outside?

He went on about this for some time until we suggested he put a sign up outside the church:

EVEN MORE INTERESTING PEOPLE INSIDE

and it all fizzled out. There is the fading, mystery of:

TNARUATSER

with an arrow pointing to absolutely nowhere, and the old sign that used to say:

PRIVATE ROOMS WITH BAT

Though we don't know the kind of bat being offered. Could there be a large black mammal hanging upside down in each private room? Or is the owner a secret cricket fan tuning in daily to Test Match Special?

Of course it is not like the old days which gave us the comforting thought of:

NICE ROOMS WITH TOILET IN GARDEN 200 ME-
TRES AWAY

with dreams of paradise and a long walk to the loo. But the connoisseur will soon make their own collection. OMELET may seem a little plain and FREE DESERT a bit dry, but a SANDWITCH is most intriguing. My own favourite is advice from the POLISE which reads NO SLEPPING ON THE BEACH, something I have never been tempted to do.

Birds

O for the wings, for the wings of a dove!
Far away, far away would I rove!

My grandmother must have known these words from Psalm 55. Many years ago, as we travelled by bus along the South Coast of England, she looked up at a bird in the sky and told me in her soft Wiltshire accent:

Oh for the wings of a seagull is more like it.

And the old lady was right. Doves are ungainly birds: like tugs battling a headwind they flap frantically to stay in the air and do not fly far. On the other hand, gulls stay aloft effortlessly and travel vast distances as they swoop and soar, dive and glide looking for food or fun. Over the years I have seen many varieties of birds on the island, especially during the seasons of migration, as birds go north in the spring and south in the autumn. Sometimes I walk to the headland outside the village where the automated shipping light is located. Battered by wind and scorched by the sun I sit with my binoculars and hope my timing is right. The small birds like to have a following wind, the large ones don't seem to care. In their time I have seen hoopoes, bee-eaters, kingfishers, stilts, plovers, cranes and even, a long way from home, an Egyptian goose. The birds that excite me most are the raptors. We have Bonelli's here and long-legged buzzards, marsh and pallid harriers and recently, in the autumn, I have seen ospreys circling high over the sea, looking for fish: elbows up in their ungainly, unmistakable style. Spring is the best time to see eagles: flying close to the sea they go directly from the cape to Vananda, a green oasis with sweet water further up the coast. Rising waves push a cushion of air above them and eagles use this cushion: they are lifted up by a wave and then, without effort or discernible use of energy, glide down before being lifted up again and repeating the operation using the waves and gravity as a horizontal moving staircase. One time I watched a large bird I thought to be an eagle heading north in this fashion. Suddenly it was attacked by a smaller bird, perhaps half its size. Following the smaller bird through my binoculars I realised that was an eagle and, focusing on the larger bird I could see it had horn-like feathers on its head. It was an eagle owl heading from Africa to the steppes of South East Europe: a huge bird capable of killing small deer; magnificent; magic; mesmerising.

One late evening in October I stood with Georgos at dusk, by the rocks in the harbour, transfixed as a pair of eagles, possibly Bonelli's, flew high above us and called to one another: *cyuk, cyuk, cyuk*, before rushing together, joining their feet and spinning round and round like children in a playground. At the last moment, nearly touching the sea, they let go and flew up, glinting in the light, to repeat the process once more. Oblivious to our presence, or knowing we offered no threat, they allowed us to watch their ritual for nearly an hour. As we returned to the shore we could hear their cries in the dark: *cyuk, cyuk, cyuk*.

From my little boat I see many birds along the coast: cormorants and shags: including the local variety with a white front, several varieties of heron: squacco, purple and grey and sometimes, as I return from fishing, a ghostly night heron passes overhead. In the spring there are cattle egrets, elegant in the wind and great and little egrets in their impossibly white plumage, also storks, spoonbills and the jet black, glossy ibis. Most surprising of all, even a little frightening, I have seen Goliath herons, *ardea goliath*, that stand one and a half metres high with a wingspan of two and a half metres. Several times I watched a pair of these rare birds as they ate cockles, limpets and crabs from the rocks. They jump in the air to take off, flap ungainly and achieve height slowly. Prehistoric and vulnerable they take circular glides to check their position before moving north, always north. Finally they moved to another island going who knows where.

We have three kinds of gull here: Adouin's, yellow-legged and Mediterranean. They can be told apart by the colour of their legs and beaks: dark legs and red beak, yellow and yellow and dark and red respectively. That's the theory. A rough sea in fading light, with spray all over your lenses complicates the issue and it is best to rely upon the jizz or flying pattern of the birds and allow instinct to lead you. Another sea based bird is Cory's shearwater. Most villagers do not differentiate the gulls nor the shearwaters from gulls, but Cory's are special. They glide for hours, centimetres above the sea, turning from side to side, almost at right angles to the surface. Cory's are flying machines: they cup their wings to form a cushion as they glide slowly above the water: sometimes they drop to sit on the sea for a few second until, lifted by the swell, they fall forward and glide down wave once again.

Sometimes their wing tips brush against the water, leaving transient circles as memorials to their passing. At a distance, as they turn, it is possible to make out the upper, dark side of the wings and then, as they turn the other way, there is a sudden show of white from under their wing. I believe this white underwing sends a signal to other Cory's who keep one eye open for food in the sea and the other eye on one another. When they see flashes of white it means changes of direction by other birds and that means food. Each evening a flock of over 200 Cory's fly past the village: far out to sea, south to north, flickering white and black against the evening sky. Until Pers, a Danish ornithologist, pointed this out, they were unseen by villagers and tourists alike. Now, each night, we look for them on the horizon. Where they are going is a mystery: the books say they nest in burrows and have a distinctive cry: gaooh-ak, gaooh-ak. Georgos thinks he has heard them at night on the east side of Saria; I think they go further north to another island. Dinos, being a village nationalist, gets angry about this:

> If they are special birds they are ours. They stay on
> Saria.

The people of the village know I am interested in birds, they tell me what they have seen and ask me questions. In common with most rural people they have no great depth of knowledge of the natural world around them. In another life I have been in close proximity to barn owls. I am used to their behaviour and the sounds they make, so when I heard: *shhh, shhh, shhh* coming from the church tower one night, I knew what to look for. And there, high up near the redundant bell, were two young birds: wings flapping, mouths open, as the parents flew around with mice and beetles and other tasty morsels. The nest, a heap of wood and leaves and pellets, would be close by. A few mornings later, some children brought me a white bundle of fluff with a fierce beak. A baby owl had fallen from the tower and fluttered down to earth on unformed wings.

We put it in a box and carried it to the *Natura* (Environmental Protection) office. I explained how to feed it cat food and how to drip water into its open beak to keep it nourished. The following day it was still alive and it was time to put it back near the nest to be looked after by its parents. We leant a long ladder against the tower and I went to fetch the bird from the office. Anna was interested in what we were doing: she loves nature and was fascinated by the idea that each adult barn owl keeps down the rat population by several hundred a year. I explained what had happened to the bird and as she lives near the church, asked if she had heard: *shhh, shhh, shhh* at night. Deadpan, she told me that she had heard the noise, but thought it was a ghost. There are still barn owls in the village; sometimes you can see them in the dark by the church. But you have to look. We also have ghosts.

Balakas

Several migrants live in the village: Albanians, Egyptians, Rumanians and an Italian. Mostly they are young men and they find work as builders or carpenters. Some of them are highly skilled. Two are Africans: tall, young, slim and very black. They are refugees from Senegal, sad to be away from home, but glad to have work even in this strange place. Thousands of refugees arrive in Europe each year, often after long and dangerous journeys. Newspapers are full of compassion when they show us the dead bodies washed up on a beach in the Canary Islands, Malta or Southern Italy, but their interest is to sell papers and they do not tell the full story.

For centuries West Africa had a thriving and sustainable fishing industry employing local, skilled young men who went out daily in their *pirogues*, drove through the surf and fished with long lines and nets. Fresh fish were sold in local markets and salted fish were sold regionally. This kind of fishing is dangerous, hard work, but the fishermen made a living and their efforts supported a local, indigenous industry: employing thousands and feeding tens of thousands. Then the fish ran out. Not in Africa, but in Europe and Japan. Governments did what governments do. They avoided the truth. They hid behind the wrongheaded belief that the seas are an abundant, limitless resource. They did not seek to preserve the fish stocks at home, instead they subsidised large companies to build huge and supposedly efficient ships which used the latest technology to roam the world catching other people's fish.

After a few million euros were deposited in discrete bank accounts, permission was granted for these factory ships to exploit the seas of West Africa. Soon the local population saw large boats off the coast: fishing and dredging, day in and day out: destroying the sea bed, the local environment and the local economy. The ships provided no work for the local people, just took away their fish. The destruction was as cruel and massive as the clear cutting of rain-forests: a crime against the environment by the haves for the haves, paid for by the have-nots. Soon the fish ran out and the ships moved on, leaving behind an unemployed and resentful population with boats and the courage and skills to roam the oceans. Now, the sea brings a new harvest: young black men and women who end up dead on the shore, or are taken into the underworld of crime and drugs and prostitution while money goes into similar, discrete, bank accounts. In different ways the scenario is repeated across the world; poor people are robbed and then blamed for being poor; a problem that will not go away and which has no solution under current economic and political structures.

Here in Greece the government seeks to alleviate the pressure on Athens by dispersing refugees away from the capital and subsidises villages who take them to do work in the local community. Our local government arranged for the Senegalese to come and stay. They are clearly athletic and one time I wondered if they were part of our new basketball team. This turned out to be prescient. They are good footballers and should be in the village team, but there was a major row with the other villages on the island who insisted that a 'one foreign player' rule should apply. So they take it in turns.

One of the Senegalese, Moustapha has become a close friend. He is impossibly beautiful with long, flexible limbs like the young Muhammad Ali. He laughs a lot. Wearing a tattered baseball cap pulled low he has a wondrous smile, but only occasionally shows his dark, intelligent eyes. Moustapha speaks his tribal language, Wolof, two other tribal languages, Swahili, French and a little English. I am teaching him Greek. How many Senegalese speak Greek? With a cockney accent. Moustapha is a sensitive man, but rather shy and finds it difficult being one of only two black people in the village:

> All eyes are on me. The only black man in the *cafeneion.*

He makes jokes about these things but, if you listen carefully, you hear the pain.

> I am black, I am *malakas.* So I am *balakas.*

Moustapha can be very funny and also perceptive. We met for coffee one morning at the Gorgona. Gabriella is a very good cook and kind to Moustapha, but one time she arrived late, obviously in a bad mood:

> Gabi is sad.

He said softly:

> Problem with the heart.

He paused:

> Problem with the head.

Then a long, delicious, pause:

> Problem with the body.

And he laughed his sad melancholic laugh. An African man far from home. A black man, but not *balakas.*

The Boatman

Nikos is a captain. A big captain. He knows boats and he knows the sea. He knows people too and cares for them. In his boat, no matter the weather, you will be safe. There was nobody with him when the following events took place some thirty years ago. He was alone. The sea was dead calm, *ladi mas leme*, like oil, we say. Nikos set off for the south, a two hour journey to the nearest town. He was in his *maouna*s, a wooden boat about six metres long with an inboard engine. Chugga, chugga, chugga and off he went. Such boats are steered by a tiller. You sit on a bench at the back, hat pulled down over your eyes, lean on the tiller and there you are. Nikos did not sit on the bench for long, he has big shoulders, strong arms, but short legs and the bench cut into them. He squatted on the bench and sat on the gunnel at the stern of the boat. The sea was calm, there was no wind and no need to keep close in to the coast. He ticked off the landmarks: Fokai, Meres, Papa Minas, Makria Punta. Five kilometres off the beach of Opsi, Nikos felt as calm as the sea and relaxed and relaxed and relaxed. He woke as he hit the water:

Splash, splutter, flap, swallow, cough, spit.

Now he was wide awake. And scared. The land was too far away for him to swim. Five kilometres is a lot and there are strong currents. He did not panic, he could not afford to, but he did some fast thinking. When you let go of the tiller of such boats it turns one way or the other and the boat goes round and round in a circle. This can be handy, but it can be dangerous: the boat can run over someone in the sea and the propeller can mash them up: so Nikos was ready when the *maounas* came back. He leant up out of the sea and grabbed the prow of the boat: he heaved himself out of the water, but a wet Nikos is a heavy object and he could not hang on. He fell back into the sea.

I have been in a similar situation, though not as dangerous. Getting into a boat after diving for fish requires a certain technique. Forget the technique and you struggle. You attempt it for a second time and the technique is better, but you are not as strong. You had better make it by the third attempt or your strength has gone and you have to swim for shore. Nikos did not have this option. He had to get into the boat at the next attempt, or drown.

All boats should have oars. Engines can break down, but men rarely do. Without an engine you can still row, still find safety. In the village we do not use rowlocks. Oars are attached to a boat with a special rope wrapped round *scarmoi*, short pieces of wood that stand vertically, two on each side. Many times *scarmoi* are broken and you see boats in the village with only two, one or even without any. Without *scarmoi* it is impossible to row a boat. Obsessively I always have four in good condition and spares when needed. Nikos is not obsessive like me, but as the boat came round again he saw there were two *scarmoi* on his side. He does not know how he got into the boat, just remembers reaching up with one hand to grab one *scarmos,* then with the other hand he took the side gunnel and helped by the movement of the boat, one leg was over the side. He paused for breath, one last heave and he was on the floor of the boat sobbing and swearing with relief and gratitude. He was cut, bloodied and bruised and his hands and shoulders hurt, but he was safe: he was going to live. Putting the engine in neutral he paused to think. He took off his shirt and jeans to dry in the sun: took the paper money out of his pocket and placed it safely on the floor of the boat, weighed down by the anchor chain. But where were his *pantofles,* his flip flops?

Over there. Bobbing in the sea with his hat. Slowly he turned the boat and returned to the site of his mishap, picked up his hat and *pantofles* and with a sigh and a laugh, but still severely shaken, headed south. This time sitting firmly on the bench.

There is a coda to this story. In the village you never know how, or who, to tell of such mishaps. Sometimes I just blurt it out, everyone laughs and that's it. Nikos has status in the village. He needs to be more circumspect. He told just one person, also called Nikos. Now this other Nikos is a sceptic, even a cynic. He didn't believe the story. Two weeks later in the same boat in the same weather the two Nikos were heading south again, the second Nikos squatting on the gunnels, much as the first had done. And...he fell asleep and fell into the sea. Luckily the other Nikos was awake and heard a splash and felt the boat lurch as the tiller was released. He took the tiller, turned the boat round and hauled his bedraggled companion out of the sea. Then the two Nikos collapsed with laughter.

One Nikos told me this story. I will not say which.

Migration

At the far north of Saria is a rock called *armeno petra*, sail rock. If you travel on the ferryboat going north, ask a villager to point it out to you: they all know where it is and many have a story to tell. In the old days it was here that oars were put away and sails were raised, so it was a sad place: a place to say farewell to the village traditions, friends and family. Emigration is not a new phenomenon for the villagers: for centuries they went away in the summer to work in Asia Minor, returning in the winter to fish and cultivate their own fields. From the First World War, the Greco-Turkish war and the exchange of populations in 1923, Asia Minor was closed to Greeks, seasonal migration became impossible and *armeno petra* ceased to be the limit of the old life and became the frontier of a new world.

The original migrants to America are dead now, but it is still possible to meet their children and their grandchildren. The earlier *chorianoi*, villagers, went to Ohio, Virginia, Pennsylvania, Indiana and Kentucky and worked as miners and builders. From around 1920, the next wave of settlers congregated in Baltimore. The names in those early days are the names you find in the Baltimore phone book and in the village today: Agapios, Dargakis, Vasiliadis, Georgakis, Lendakis, Balaskas, Prearis, Philipakis, Protopapas and Hapsis. There were many reasons for leaving the village: poverty, even starvation, or ambition and a sense of adventure, or to follow a loved one, or answer the call of a relative who needed help. One old man even told me a spirit came to him in the night and told him he had to go. Whatever the reason, the villagers were still *chorianoi* and broadly led the same lives in America as they would in Greece. Even today they celebrate Easter and *panegyri* in the same way as they would in the village and in the evenings you will see the men gathered in *cafeneia* telling stories about the fish they caught and the girls they didn't, or maybe the other way round. Nobody from the village wants to work for another family, they want to run their own business and in America most end up with small building companies, restaurants or bars. Inevitably they succeed and the business grows to be passed on to children and grandchildren. Go to Baltimore today and you will find rich and powerful entrepreneurs: villagers with broad American accents: products of the American dream who respect their parents and grandparents, talk of *to chorio* and talk of returning. Think of *The Godfather*. Think of *The Wire*. Take out the stereotype and some of the crime and you will be close to the truth.

Some migrants return in the summer: overfed and loud, with boisterous children and plenty of money. Then there is talk in the village of too much Coca Cola and a smugness among those who never left. Some villagers come back after ten or twenty years and invest their savings in a taxi business or a new hotel. Others come back to retire and go fishing. Often there is a deeper reason, even ideological. Sitting with a friend outside his restaurant by the sea, one night when the *sirocco* was blowing, he told me the following:

> I was in a friend's house in Canada. It was just before Christmas about eight years ago. My friend was phoning his daughter in Florida. I heard her voice.
>
> Say hi to mom.

And I thought "Just before Christmas and all she offers is, say hi to mom?" And decided there and then:

> I want outta here. Driving home with my wife I told here my feelings and she agreed with me so we left America and came back home.

He looked into the dark as he sipped a small *raki*. Putting down his glass he turned to look at me:

> I want my children to speak English and think Greek.

Speak English and think Greek sums up the ambition of many parents from *to chorio*.

Most of those who return have money in their pocket: enough to buy a car, or a boat, refurbish their family home and start a small business. But their lives and their standing have changed. They will be referred to, though not to their faces, as the American and their names will be Americanised: Georgos becomes George, Michaelis is Mike and Nikos transmogrifies to Nick. There is a slight, but discernible innuendo that those who left are different to those that stayed. The stigma attached to emigration surfaces in stories, ballads and *mantinades*, but rarely in fights or arguments and it is a stigma that is fading; more money, easier travel and even new technologies enable the diaspora to maintain strong links with the homeland. I have known young people commute to America two or three times a year and seen mobile phones used to send sound and pictures from village festivals across the Atlantic, while the John Hopkins hospital in Baltimore remains a first choice for many villagers.

God is Great

Drinking *cafe latte*, one morning in the Gorgona, I watch Kosmas sitting quietly in the corner writing *mantinades*. I start to think about lunch. That's how tough it is here.

Along comes Marina, Georgos' mother. She has a bowl of *patsas* for me. I will spare the squeamish, but for the anatomically minded try googling *patsas*. I thank her profusely, she scolds me as usual and tells me:

> Don't bother with *avgolemono* sauce, just heat it up
> and eat with good bread and a squeeze of lemon.

I set off homeward with my bowl, wondering where I can get bread from and whether it is worth climbing to the top of the hill behind my house to pick lemons. It is windy and as I turn down the little lane by the church I am surprised to see a lemon rolling towards me: small but juicy and perfect. I pocket the lemon.

As I walk past the Anixis restaurant, Vassillis starts shouting at me:

> *Ella dw ella dw.* Come here. Come here.

Vassilis is a big man. When he shouts, you listen. So I go close.

> Take this bread, *artos*, from the church. There was a
> festival this morning.

I laugh as he gives me a large lump of fresh, crusty bread:

Why are you laughing?

I tell him of the *patsas* and the search for lemon and bread. He tells me:

O theos enai megalos.

And surely it is true:

God is great.

A Village Priest

Papa Minas is a lovely man. My children, when they were children, met him first and explained that they had met a priest who spoke perfect English and also German, Italian and French. His English is not perfect, but certainly very good and full of surprises. One day, amid the usual mayhem of the ferry boat arrival on the harbour, he wandered past me muttering:

Much ado about nothing.

Deeply but quietly religious, he has a waspish sense of humour, a cute eye for village life and a profound love of nature. When I arrived in the village he was one of the few who were interested in birds and flowers and the natural landscape; we often walked together in the mountains and he showed me orchids and shrubs and wild vegetables and fruits. One spring day, many years ago, we were looking at a flowering bush. Spotting a bee he slowly leant forward, picked it up, looked at it carefully before putting it back down, saying:

One of mine, I think.

To this day I do not know if he was joking, but that's how I discovered he was a beekeeper as well as a farmer. He loves the wild places and he loves servicing the chapels strategically and beautifully located in this historic landscape. Celebrating the name day of *Agias Georgos* we were at the *monastiri* of that name at the top of the valley above Vananda. The structure is white and simple and carefully located for meditation and the worship of God: steep cliffs and mountains are all around and over the pine trees there is a sweeping view to the sea. In recent memory this was home to monks and hermits.

With a provocative look in his eye the *Papas* asked me if I would like to live there and together we looked at the little hermitage. It is a plain building with a wooden *sofa*, there is water, but no electricity, the room is high enough to be cool in the summer but the winters would be cold and hard and I am not made to be a hermit. One detail is still with me. In the centre of the ceiling hung a primitive chandelier containing ancient light bulbs. The old people collected them when they were thrown up by the sea and, anticipating the arrival of electricity, used to hang them in their houses as decorations. That day Papa Minas sported a Sony Walkman given to him, I suspect, by one of his daughters. The earphones looked rather strange with his priestly robes and he explained to me with a laugh that he wanted to be the first priest in space. The location is made for music and imagining Karajan and Beethoven I asked what music was to his taste. He told me:

Petula Clark.

We got him the tapes of her greatest hits.

Notwithstanding his talents Papas Minas is a modest man. I know little of the Orthodox church and made a mistake once by addressing him simply as Papa. He explained gravely:

There is only one Papa and I have no ambitions in that direction.

I never used to go to church until the *Papas* asked me why not. I told him I was not a Christian. His response was immediate:

Do you think we are?

So I started to attend the services.

Discussing stereotypes one day, I explained I try to avoid the temptation to fall back on the template rather than the individual. I illustrated the point crudely:

Tourists think all Greeks are Zorba the Greek.

He was thoughtful for a while before responding with a twinkle:

Yes, but all Greeks are Zorba the Greek.

And I knew what he meant.

Another time, he was in a conversation with a group of Germans. I overheard them ask him if the Greeks have an expression like the Spanish *mañana*. With a deadpan expression and exquisite timing he told them:

Here, we are not so precise.

I do not have the temerity to attempt a biography of the man as I am sure it would lead me round and round in a labyrinth. I know he was a shepherd and he doesn't like travelling by boat and he used to be some kind of worker priest in Germany, but little else. His politics are sophisticated: when we first met he was reading Bury my Heart at Wounded Knee by Dee Brown and for sure he is a green and celebrated the deposing of a reactionary local politician (and there are plenty of those) by telling me it was July 14th (Bastille day) in the village. Voting figures are given for the village, party by party in national elections. Normally the figure is two to one in favour of the socialists over the right wing and with commendable discipline, no other party is represented. One year I noticed one solitary vote for KKE, the communists. I asked Papa Minas who he thought it was and he told me:

I don't know, but someone in my family I think.

And laughed gently as he walked away.

But he is a man of faith, not a politician. I was out of the village on September 11th 2001 and returned a few days later. The women were horrified at the mass murder and destruction, but few men showed sympathy for the dead and damaged of New York. Some declared that the Americans now know what it is like, or they had it coming to them. Unanimously they seemed to think it was a Jewish conspiracy and believed no Jews went to work in the Twin Towers that day.

My anger at this nonsense must have shown and soon after I was in conversation with the *Papas*. Our priest is also a village man and not immune to the pressures and prejudices of our society. Whilst calm and sensible he was also very angry and the reason was:

These murderers did it in the name of God.

A sentiment I have not heard elsewhere, but one which, amidst all the turmoil, seemed to define the man and express his character.

Easter

The village celebrates many festivals. To the outsider they are a spectacle: something to look at, photograph and film: something to capture, take home and show to friends. For the *chorianoi*, the villagers, they are part of the rich texture of life: the warp and weft of village society. Songs and dances, feasts and worship are important emotional outlets, but they also offer the opportunity for obligations to be honoured, debts to be paid, the possibilities of marriage to be explored and family ties to be strengthened.

Many festivals are associated with Christianity and the most important of these is Easter. The forty days of Lent are strictly observed by the faithful and disciplined who abstain from meat, olive oil, fish and alcohol. These are not easy observances among those who work with their hands and the tempo of village life noticeably slows. By *Megalo Paraskevi*, Big (i.e. Good) Friday, the mood is sombre and the village silent. Lights are lowered at night as a small, candlelit procession circulates the village, stopping at houses of the recently dead to allow prayers to be said for the departed. *Megalo Sabato*, begins slowly with a Church service in the late morning and much restless pacing about. This is a day of fasting and tension: the people are hungry, they are on edge and impatiently await the resurrection of Christ, joy and rich food. The evening service starts around 10 p.m. with a small choir: just two or three men, singing Byzantine hymns from the mediaeval liturgy. Soon the devout, the bereaved, the guilty and those seeking advancement begin to arrive: women in their finest clothes, men in dark suits, children, scrubbed and shining.

The atmosphere is thick with incense and the smell of beeswax candles. Neighbours greet one another, admire clothes or jewellery, comment on how the children have grown, ask about relatives and how it was in Rhodos, Athens or Baltimore. Amidst the hubbub the church fills and the *Papas* goes about his work: Christ will be born again: he will arise in triumph and the congregation will be brought to ecstasy. Spurred on by the *Papas*, the music, interwoven with the spoken word, graphically tells the Easter story in passionate, gory detail.

Outside, across the alleyway from the church, there are worn steps leading to an empty house: one of the oldest in the village. Sometimes I sit there in the dark, listening to music sung before there was electricity in the village, before the road came, before wheels were used: music from the time of pirates, fear and superstition: music from the days when there was only one book in the village: *to biblio*: the book, the Bible. I hear the priest acting out vivid scenes and hear chants of supplication, pain and suffering. He is a good man and this is a hard time. He feels the nails, begs forgiveness and suffers desolation.

There are many duties leading up to Easter and Papas Minas has been working hard for forty days and is close to exhaustion. In the dark there are fireworks, some of them big, for Greeks celebrate with loud bangs and the younger men of the village are impatient for Christ to arise: they want to impress their friends, show off to the girls and party. Carelessly they mix the profane with piety: sometimes dynamite is used and sometimes the priest stops the service and steps outside to tell these wild young men that unless they behave he will not announce the resurrection and their family will be delayed in the church and supper will be late. If the young lads are too rowdy and a police-

man is in the village, he may appear in uniform and shyly
and discreetly hover in the yard near the church door to try
and ensure tranquillity. But things can get out of hand.
One time, rival gangs were fighting it out with rockets and
bangers so fiercely that the unfortunate policeman had to
hold up a flag of truce to allow women, children and myself to go to our respective homes.

Inside the church it is crowded and smoky with incense;
men stand on one side of the aisle and young women on
the other. The older ladies arrived early and pushed themselves upstairs onto the balcony to have the best view of
the priest playing his flock like an old rock star: orchestrat-
ing emotions and refusing to announce the saviour is saved
until he, the *Papas*, is ready. They see the strain on his
handsome face, hear the pain, the love and joy in his voice
and finally feel the ecstasy of the words:

> *Christos Anesty, Christos Anesty, Christos Anesty.* Christ
> is risen. Christ is risen. Christ is risen.

Now there is a mass exodus from the church, hand-
shakes and greeting, shouts and screams as the ground
shakes with massive explosions, flares are lit and rockets
fired. Girls who want to get married and children who want
good luck, cup the flames of candles as they walk slowly
through the mayhem with their family group: old ladies in
black, mothers in finery and fathers warily looking around.
If the candle is still burning as they reach home then wishes
will be granted. In the houses tables are laid with the best
linen and cutlery: wine and retsina is poured and for the
old men, *ouzo* or whisky. Tomorrow will be the day for *ofto*:
lamb stuffed with rice and herbs from the mountains, but
today is the time for *margaritsa*: a thick, strong soup of
sheep offal and bits and pieces.

For days now sheep have been strung up and slaugh-
tered all over the village. Encountering the reality of the

village food chain for the first time at the age of four and excited by the spectacle, my granddaughter once offered, without irony, to show me where they turn sheep into lamb. Everything of the carcass is used: intestines, lungs, liver and feet. Small fires have been burning in the streets as the heads are burnt and then stewed and all of it goes into the pot. After forty days of fasting such a rich potage gives a powerful hit to the system. Year after year I eat this special meal with the same family and year after year I take my leave, a little too early, so as to walk alone through the empty streets a few hours before dawn and feel that Christ is risen and all is well in the village.

Soon the parties will begin.

Easter Week

In the week that follows Easter there are many celebrations: they are important to the people of the village and private as too many outsiders would mean the delicate balance between performance and ritual, friendship, rivalry and fun would be destroyed. My favourite celebration is a simple little festival, nothing much more than a village picnic, but its origins are pre-Christian. The day starts with a parade of church icons around the village followed by a short, joyful service in the church. The icons are then 'auctioned' in the church yard where prominent villagers compete to offer money to the church for one year's nominal responsibility for each icon.

Depending on their piety, guilt, wealth and whose turn it is, bids are made and the icons are awarded. There follows a procession, north along the coast, through the trees along the cliff top, to a small beach with a sweet water spring. At the front of the procession is the priest, happy now that Easter is drawing to a close, as he strides ahead, singing hymns. Following him are the local worthies, carrying their borrowed icons, young men and finally women and girls in their *kavai* and traditional finery; the trill of laughter mixing with the squeak of their boots. Older people come by truck and if the sea is calm, by boat. When the procession reaches the beach, the priest blesses the spring and then the icons, *ouzo* is poured and ancient songs are sung to the water that brings life. I am told these songs are a thousand years old, but the sentiment is much older and comes from a time when the people needed rain in the

winter to survive and were compelled to show their gratitude to the water spirits. Rain was a matter of life and death
in those days: if it rained the crops would grow, children
could eat and the village multiply. Drought meant crop
failure, hunger and death.

After the blessings we sit around in little family groups
under the tamarisk trees and eat *ofto* left over from Easter
Sunday, and home baked bread with salty *sardelles* and
goats cheese, sweetmeats and delicacies. Sometimes music
is played and if there are enough young people, they form
a circle and dance soft and easy, round and round to the
hypnotic sound of the lute and the trill of the *lyra*. If there
is romance in the air a young man will sing a ballad or two,
the high, controlled notes full of the mystery of love. And
then, as with many events in the village, the festivities come
to a stuttering halt and for no discernible reason, everyone
goes home.

Two days later there is a *panegyri*, a festival, for the village. First a church service, where the best suits and boots
and finery are on display again and the air is thick with the
smell of mothballs and incense while the soft sound of the
sea is punctured by the whoosh and crack of fireworks.
Coming out of the church there is *ouzo* and *arto*, the spicy
church bread in loaves the size of cartwheels. The church
yard is full of villagers greeting friends and neighbours and
family members from Canada, America, Rhodes or Athens.
Kronia polla, they say, many years, and kiss and shake hands
and pose for formal photographs. The women are beautiful, the men play bit parts from low grade B-movies and the
children are spoilt. Somehow, even with the whole village
in this crowded space, neighbours, or family members who
don't speak to one another, still don't speak to one another, as they thread in and out of the throng avoiding the
eyes they don't want to see and the hands they will not
shake.

Somehow, we drift down the marble stairs to the village hall, *to megaron*. We sit together on benches, facing one another across tables loaded with bread and olives and morsels of fish and goat's liver. Reflecting the division in the church men are on one side of the hall and women, children and the odd tourist are on the other. The overwhelming impression, as the entire village sits down to eat together, is one of solidarity, but look carefully and you will note the seating arrangements reflect the choreography of avoidance, driven by ancient or contemporary feuds.

Drinks are poured: coca cola, *ouzo*, *restsina*, or for those intending to celebrate hard, whisky. Glasses are clinked and toasts are made while the women and church elders serve the food. All morning Elias has been standing in the sun by a huge casserole, stirring mutton stew with a long wooden spoon. Large chunks of meat with chips and rice and a token salad are placed before each of us, hungry or not. At the head table sit the local politicians, a bishop and assorted priests. Of course we get a speech from the bishop. He tells us what a wonderful place the village is and how lucky we are and thanks us for our hospitality. Then we have Byzantine hymns. Everybody joins in and we sing a verse or two before taking our forks and tapping plates louder and louder, until the hymn is stopped and another starts. An hour passes and the bishop has to go: we stand to wish him *kalo taxidi* and the lunch is over. But not the celebrations.

A group of old men head for the *cafeneion* and whisky. From now on the game is to drink small shots steadily until the party finishes. One of the men will be recognised as *meraklis* and he will informally direct the proceedings. In recent years this has been Manolis, a powerfully built, but gentle man and a renowned musician. Instruments appear: *lyra* and *lauto* but not, as yet, my favourite, the *tsambouna* or bagpipe. The *megaron* has emptied and been cleaned and a group of tables arranged for the next act. The men move back there with bottles and instruments and the weight of years. They are about to undertake an emotional *katharsis* or cleansing. There are several whisky bottles on the table: Cutty Sark and Johnnie Walker and from a returning villager, a bottle of Canadian Club. Glasses are filled, the table tapped, good health is proffered, instruments are tuned and the *mantinades* begin.

Mantinades are a local verse form, two lines of fifteen syllables with strict metre, they are appreciated best when improvised. First the oldest man welcomes the ensemble, makes jokes about his age and tells us how grateful he is to still be here. The atmosphere is light and easy, they are friends, relatives, villagers together. But they are here for more than fun. They want to clear their minds, bare their souls, cry and feel better. This is a small village and this group are its heart: everyone knows everything about everybody else, but all year long deep feelings are hidden, face is saved and mouths are kept shut. Now they will be open.

The *meraklis* leads, but this is a group activity: these are comrades, villagers, family. Shots of whisky keep coming as do the *mantinades* the camaraderie and the support. After a while one of the ensemble is coaxed to sing. They know he has a problem, they know he has prepared a *mantinada* to express his feelings and now they will lead him to open his heart. This is a profound and moving experience. I am privileged to be here: I do not belong, but I am invited. In the West we never tell the truth in public: we hide, dissemble, lie, make jokes and avoid the truth.

These men are going to sing of their deepest feelings, they are going to tell us their pain. Of course there are matters which are easy to share: the death of a mother, sickness, the loss of a son: socially acceptable, commonly understood feelings, but in this bare room, with the simple rhythm of old tunes and the subtle use of alcohol the men fall into a trance and tell us the difficult things: I was sick: the doctor gave me tablets and I became addicted to these tablets or, my son got married to a girl away from here without my permission: I think it a mistake and my heart is broken and so on. One time a returned villager, now a successful doctor in America, sang of his wealth and fame, but the ensemble knew there was something else and after many, many hours finally forced him to reveal his problem with a *mantinada* which told us he had botched an operation and killed a patient. Of course there were tears, not only from the singer, but the others who sing the chorus to the song. And also from me. These are my friends, they show their vulnerability and I do the same.

Aristotle explained that catharsis not only cleanses the soul, but more importantly its exercise enables the emotions to expand and people to become human. The singing, coaxing and cleansing continue for many hours until emotions are exhausted. By now women and children have joined us. They bring food and drink, place it on the table before us and sit discretely at the back of the hall. It is dark outside and suddenly the music stutters and stops, the ensemble stands, tables are moved and chairs are placed on tables in the centre of the room. The *meraklis* rinses his hand in whisky to ease the arthritic pain, takes his *lyra* and sits above us. Then, with a change of tempo, the music begins again, old men take the hands of a daughter or grand daughter and begin to dance briskly in a circle around the hall.

As the hall fills the circle of dancers grows and the evening rolls on; there are more than a hundred in the line now, hand to handkerchief to hand, with boots clumping, jewellery clanking and bodies swaying back and forward to the strum of the strings and the slide of the bow. The lead, male, dancer twirls and leaps, slaps both feet twice while in the air and is down again and up and away. *Ella, ella, ella;*

ella, ella, ella. *Tsambouna* players have joined the musicians, two of them, driving the music and rocking the dancers. I have a bottle of whisky in my hand. I stand at the head of the line, fill the cap and offer it to each dancer as they pass. A cap for them, a cap for me. All the men drink and some of the women and suddenly the bottle is empty and I am back in my seat again with the rhythm pounding as the village celebrates.

Two *loutes* provide the rhythm, a *lyra* keeps the melody and the *tsambouna* players honk and squeak like young John Coltranes. The musicians pound their feet on the large wooden tables; bang, bang, bang, bang: just off the beat but not syncopated. Bang, bang, bang, bang. Bang, bang, bang, bang. *Ella, ella, ella; ella, ella, ella.* In the midst of the mayhem Karellas appears: his pony tail swinging, a bottle of whisky in his hand and a wicked grin on his face. Now he stands at the head of the line, bottle in one hand and a glass in the other. The cap has gone spinning into the night and it is a double for you a double for me, a treble for you, a treble for me and on and on until the whole line are swaying and dancing like demons and Vallaskas is on his feet waving his arms and at the top of his voice: *ella, ella, ella; ella, ella, ella.* Bang, bang, bang, bang. Bang, bang, bang, bang.

On and on and on. I ask the time at 11.30 p.m. the next I know it is 3.30 a.m. and I stagger off to bed. Immediately I fall sleep, but three hours later I am awake again. The music still fills the village and I am still drunk, but something terrible has happened; I cannot think in English: only in Greek. A lifelong ambition to learn the language has been achieved with one bottle of whisky, but I have lost my mother tongue. I panic and think, in what seems to be perfect Greek:

Just one word. If I could only say one word I will speak English again.

But I cannot.

Mercifully I sleep again. When I wake, it is afternoon and I can speak English once more. The village is quiet, but the rhythm stays with me. *Ella, ella, ella; ella, ella, ella.*

Morena

There are strange creatures in the sea: some beautiful, some ugly; all have their place in the underwater hierarchy. The only one I hate is the *morena* or *smyrna*, known in England as moray eel. In the waters I dive *morena* reach more than a metre in length and weigh several kilos of hard muscle and sharp teeth. According to Wikipedia they have a second set of jaws in their throat, the pharyngeal jaws, which also possess teeth. When they are feeding *morena* launch these jaws into the mouth, where they grasp their prey and drag it into the throat and digestive system. Moray eels are the only animal known to use pharyngeal jaws to actively capture and restrain prey. Wikepedia helpfully adds:

> Larger morays are capable of seriously wounding humans.

The first *morena* I saw in the sea was off Papa Minas beach. In those days I used to snorkel naked; not a pretty sight even then. I was alone, on the north side heading towards the shore in about two metres of water. I felt some presence. I looked around, but saw nothing until I looked down. Underneath me, swimming on its side like a long, mottled ribbon, was a large *morena* looking up and showing teeth in a threatening grin. I was not a good swimmer in those days and had never water planed, but I came out of the sea so fast I did not stop swimming until I was half way up the beach. Since then I have always worn trunks.

Of course I asked about these creatures before I went alone to dive and shoot fish. I was reassured by Georgos:

> They stay in their holes and never attack a humans if they see all your body

Georgos knows about these things: he once shot a fish which went under a rock, he left his gun down there, came to the surface and dived again, put his hand under the rock to pull out the fish and had his index finger shredded by a hidden *morena*. On the surface the blood spurted half a metre high. He got in his boat, wondered what to do, lit a cigarette and cauterised the wound before heading back to the village for medical treatment. His finger still has dozens of thin, narrow, white scars.

I was not afraid when I went diving for the first time by myself. The day was going well; my weights were adjusted, the mask did not let in water and the balloon, pulled by a line attached to my spear gun, followed me smoothly. I headed north among the rocks after Kalamnia. I shot a few fish and threaded them onto the line as I swam along the coast. I saw a good sized *scarros*, dived, shot the fish and surfaced. I was struggling to detach it from the harpoon when, ten metres in front of me, a large *morena* came out from under a rock, headed to the surface and turned in my direction. It was probably heading for the fish, but I feared for my face. The spear gun was not loaded and the fish was still on the prongs so the *morena* did not seem impressed as I poked at it, just made a grab for my fish. Suddenly, I was on my back and kicking out with my flippers while swearing underwater in my best cockney. Shouting under the sea is a difficult art. I swallowed water, coughed, cleared the snorkel, righted myself and, as the blinding white bubbles cleared, saw the *morena* had gone. And so had my fish.

Another time, another meal, this time an octopus: a big octopus. I spotted it, chose the right angle, dived, shot the creature, agitated the harpoon to detach it from its hole and surfaced. There are things you have to do to an octopus to ensure it is dead, but to fully understand you would have to be well acquainted with octopus anatomy so I will not go into details. I threaded the dead animal on the line and went on my way through sepia tinted water.

The day was windy and my balloon was flying all over the surface of the sea. All of a sudden the line was round my neck. To compound matters the line caught my snorkel, bending it under the surface. I had no air and as I fought to untangle myself, events turned nasty. A *morena*, attracted by the smell of the octopus' ink sac, took hold of the creature in its jaws and headed off, pulling the line tight round my throat. I grabbed the line, spat out the snorkel and spat out water before taking a few deep breaths and adjusting the snorkel again. I took the line in my hand and could feel and see the *morena* as it tried to escape with its prey or, to be precise, my prey. I pulled the line towards me until the *morena* was close enough for me to stab it with my harpoon. I poked the ugly creature and it turned and fled, leaving my octopus intact, though slightly frayed and me spluttering and out of breath and more than a little pissed off.

Relaying this story to Manolis, at the *Para Thin Alos* restaurant, he told me that, as an eight year old child, he had been with his father in Saria. Sitting on a rock, with his feet in the sea, he fished with a line for *scarros,* using crab as bait. As he caught fish, he cleaned them and the water round his feet was red with blood and scales and guts. Suddenly there was a swirl in the water, he felt something brush along the bottom of his feet and saw a huge *morena* appear. The water was now full of blood and he screamed as the pain hit him. His father rushed over to lift him off the rock and out of the water as blood spouted from deep cuts on his heels. He was seriously injured and loosing blood fast. The nearest doctor was two hours away by boat, but these were the old people and knew how to solve problems. In those days all the men wore *stivania,* the high sided boots made from soft goat's skin. They scraped suede off their boots with a sharp knife, made a poultice and tied it to the young boy's feet with rags. The bleeding stopped, his life was saved and a lesson learned.

Morena are powerful, frightening creatures with an aura approaching mystery. Sometimes they come out of the water. I shot an octopus one time and was lying on a beach, warming and dozing, when I suddenly felt my spear gun being dragged out of my hand and down the beach. A *morena* had come two metres up the beach, had my supper between its jaws and was slithering backwards to the sea. I had to kick it with my bare feet before it let go of the octopus and escaped. Perhaps the ability to spend time out of water has led to one of the strangest folk mythologies of the village. Some people here believe that one night a year, in high summer, *morena* come out of the water and mate with snakes on the beach. I know little of the sex life of snakes and *morena*, nor their equipment, so exactly what puts what, where and how, is a mystery, but clearly, different species cannot mate: although my faith was shaken when I saw a snake in the sea. It may have been dead, but sea snakes are poisonous and I didn't get close enough to see if it was breathing, but it was definitely a snake.

One devilish ability of *morena* is the capacity to tie themselves into knots. I have never seen this happen, but two fishermen who dive to fish, tell me they have. *Morena* love octopus and octopus are strong creatures whose suckers are a major defensive weapon. I am more than 90 kilos and strong, but if I catch a one kilo octopus on a fishing line and it takes hold of the side of my boat I cannot pull it off. I have to wait for it to try to swim away before I flick it into the boat and deal with it there. Octopus live on the sea bed under rocks, or in holes. If discovered by *morena* they cling to the side of the hole with their suckers. The *morena* sinks its teeth deeply into its prey to cause maximum damage and at the same time twists its own tail into a simple over-hand knot. It then slides the knot down its own body until it reaches the rock where the *morena* uses it like a shoulder, to add leverage to the struggle. It can still take a long time to pull out the octopus and often the struggle is abandoned and the *morena* takes off with an octopus leg between its jaws. A devilish scene for a devilish creature.

Where do you live?

I am lucky. I live in two places. Both are beautiful, easy, calm places to live. One is in the hills in Wales: nearly a kilometre from the nearest road, two from my nearest neighbour, six from the nearest shop. I live there with barn owls and tawny owls, buzzards, sparrow hawks, passerines, wild cats, pole cats, squirrels, stoats and foxes. I go to the pub and hear Welsh spoken, I sit by the fire, hold my pint and dream. A few years ago my son lived there too. He was a young man, just starting out after university and he needed support while looking for a job, so he signed on to register as unemployed. He gave them my address. The civil servant said they would send a cheque. He waited. The postman came; no cheque. He waited; the postman came again. Again no cheque. After five days he phoned them and was told:

> We do not send out cheques until we have visited the claimant in his home. Can we have your address?

He gave them the address again:

Cyffylliog, Denbighshire.

We tried to find it, but could not. What is the number of the house?

The house has no number. It only has a name.

What is the name of the street?

There is no street.

There was a pause at the other end of the line as the caller tried to puzzle out what to do:

We will try and find you again.

If you tell me when you are coming I will come to the road and meet you:

We can't do that. It must be a surprise.

Perhaps they tried again, or not, but they never found him. Eventually he scraped enough money together and came to Diafani to live with his old father. He phoned them from the public phone outside Gabriella's: the one you cannot stand up in because they raised the level of the street and did not raise the level of the phone box. Perfect for children and those of us on our knees:

I am in Greece.

We can't visit you there.

And they didn't. And he never got any money. So much for the welfare state.

The other place I live is Greece. My address is easy: Diafani, Karpathos. That's it. Simple. Except when you are dealing with outsiders. I wanted to be connected to the internet; surprisingly Greece has a modern telecoms system, one of the best in Europe. It could be done:

You will be connected as soon as the money is cleared. How would you like to pay?

I dictate the credit card numbers, the dates and so on, feeling how civilised it is to live in Greece. Until they ask for my address:

That's easy. Diafani, Karpathos.

That's not an address.

Oh yes it is.

What is the number of the house?

My house does not have a number.

What is the name of the street?

We don't have streets.

But we must have an address.

Then some lateral thinking. The man from the company tries to be helpful. He speaks slow, clear English:

What is your address in Britain?

There is a pause and:

Why are you laughing?

After a while I manage to explain and he laughed too. Eventually we found a way: there was a compromise, I invented a house number and invented the name of a street, paid my money and was connected to the internet. In Greece they find a place for you: even if you don't have a number: or a street. But it helps to live at No 1 *Vounara* (Big mountain).

And then came tourists

The first postwar tourist to the village was an American writer called John Collins who came in 1946. He was offered hospitality by the Balaskas family in their house by the sea and they remember him sitting at a table in the evening, writing in the soft glow of an oil lamp and the phut phut of its ancient mechanism. In the sixties and seventies there were visitors from northern Europe, mainly Denmark and Sweden, with a handful of Germans and the occasional American. Famous names who came include Kevin Andrews who stayed several times in the '60's and is fondly remembered; I wrote about him in *American Ikaros-The Search for Kevin Andrews*. Willard Manus, author of *This Way to Paradise: Dancing on the Tables,* came in the eighties with his family. The book is a delicious memoir of a thirty year stay in Rhodes. In Diafani they stayed with the Niotis family, and remember snorkelling and catching fish and going to a funny little man (Minas) to get Willard's hair cut.

Now we have many tourists, some of whom, to the amusement of the local people, claim to have discovered the place. There have always been tourists here, even in ancient times. Homer supposedly visited the island, indelicately named it Crapathos and described it as an island of winds. Strabo and Ptolemy were more likely visitors. Then came priests and pirates, adventurers, conquerors and settlers, while Syrians, Saracens, Turks, Italians, Germans, Indians and British swept in and out with the tides of history. Visitors who wrote about the island in the 19th and 20th

century include Mr and Mrs Theodore Bent, Richard
Dawkins and more recently Robert Liddell.

On August 2nd 1877, the English traveller and amateur
archaeologist James Theodore Bent married an extraordi-
nary Irishwoman: Mabel Virginia Anna Hall-Dare. Mabel
was 31, Theodore 25, and within a few months they had
embarked on a pattern of annual trips that continued for
20 years. In 1884 they visited Karpathos. Much later Mabel
published an account of their journeys: *The Travel Chroni-
cles of Mrs J Theodore Bent, 1883 -1898*. Written with a light
hand the couple come across as adventurous and inquisitive Victorians dealing with rogues, ragamuffins and bed-
bugs with humour, aplomb and middle class accents. In the
early spring of 1884 they travelled from Rhodes in the bows
of a *caique*. Their destination was the port of Pigadia, but
the northeast wind was so strong the following waves
broke over the stern of the *caique* and the captain was un-
willing to risk the east side of Karpathos. Instead he turned
west through the straits of Steno between Karpathos and
Saria. After a 9 hour voyage the couple arrived cold and wet
in Tristomo, a sheltered lagoon on the west side of Karpathos. Tristomo was still inhabited in those days, though
the Bents considered it to be a ruinous place. All around
they only saw steep rocks. From these they chose two of
the softest to sleep on while the Greeks slept all in a heap.

The following morning the *caique* set off for Pigadia,
north at first then east through the unusually calm straits.
After Steno they turned south but, probably at Alona, were
hit by gusts of wind which took the foresail and mast overboard and tore a hole in the bows of the boat. The captain
had seen enough bad weather, decided to abandon all
hope of Pigadia and left the Bents at Diafani. Modern day
visitors would sympathise with their next move:

We breakfasted in the open air.

A pleasant experience even in a cold northerly, but it must have been a sunny day. It being too rough for a *caique*, they followed local logic and hired a smaller boat, a *maounas* with a crew of four, in which they were rowed to Pigadia. The journey took 7 hours during which the crew sang ballads and *mantinades*. The Bents travelled around the south of the island for two weeks, arriving on March 27th at Spoa. On the 28th (Big Saturday of the Greek Easter) they set off up the spine of the island in a mule train bound for Olymbos. They found the donkey track washed away in many places while mules and donkeys went wild, packs became undone and various tins of sardines were lost. After many hours they arrived at Olymbos. They had a letter of introduction, but the house they were offered was filthy and occupied by:

a dirty priest and his wife.

The priest's name was Protopapas. He has many descendants. After looking around the village and protracted negotiation they rented the school teacher's house. Offered hospitality everywhere they went they were amused to be asked if they came from a Christian country. The following day they stumbled upon a local parliament discussing taxes and boundaries. Think of today's *cafeneion* on a larger scale: there were 80 men present on benches or sitting cross legged on the floor. Often they rose up and rushed at each other with threatening gestures, requiring two soldiers to separate them. In between skirmishes the men chatted to one another and took lights from cigarettes in a friendly manner while the schoolmaster took notes. When he announced agreement had been reached, the fighting started all over again.

The next day the Bents went to camp at Vroukounta and hoisted the Union Jack over their tent. Supper was sheep's head soup with *drilla*, sour cream, and fried liver. I have eaten the same food in the same place. Over the next few days they directed excavations and took many pretty objects, most of which ended up in the British Museum. They returned to Olymbos for a night and the following morning trekked down from Olymbos to Diafani. In the days before global warming and the urge to wash motor cars caused the water table to fall, a river ran along the valley for six months of the year. This necessitated the use of an upper footpath, still visible today, rather than the summer, or lower, path that tourists use. The Bents had to take the upper path, there was an accident and some of their belongings fell into the torrent.

In Diafani they stayed in the house of the Olymbos priest and an old lady, Hadji Mangaphou, cooked for them. It was the week following Easter and there was much dancing and feasting. Like all good tourists they spent a few days writing their journals and reading books. The watching villagers were bemused and wondered why anyone should read a book and why, if rich enough, anyone would want to write, an activity they considered hard work. Villagers often ask me the same questions. Off the Bents sailed to Saria: Mabel steered, Theodor baled the leaky boat and villagers rowed: still singing, no doubt. They found Palatia to be a pleasant place, camped up the valley near the chapel and ate supper from a table laid on the capital of a pillar: still to be found in the same spot and used for the same purpose on the name day of the chapel. They returned to Olymbos, visited Steno and stayed a few days in Vroukounta again, then on to Tristomo and Diafani where they took a *caique* to Pigadia followed by a steamer to Crete and on to Kythira, Malta and home for another year.

The British archaeologist Richard MacGillivray Dawkins (24 October 1871 - 4 May 1955) visited Karpathos in the early summer of 1903 and published his findings, Notes from Karpathos, later that year. He came to study the antiquities and the dialect and crammed an enormous amount of work into his three week stay. Much taken with the island he considered the retired position offered a favourable opportunity of study.

Luckier than the Bents, Dawkins set off from Crete in such a calm that his boat had to be rowed along the eastern shore in a dead flat sea. Still in Crete they anchored for the night off the beautiful coast of Cavo Sidhero, a slight breeze sprang up in the morning and they sailed to Phiniki on the west coast of Karpathos. Dawkins explored the south of the island then gradually headed north, commenting on the pots, people and antiquities he observed on the way. A charming aspect of Notes from Karpathos is the delicate drawings with details of pottery basins, doors of ancient monasteries, complicated wooden locks, windmills, olive presses and the wild landscape. Dawkins was much impressed with the wooden locks. He even saw some of these *mantalos* in Avlona and Olymbos. I have yet to see one, but expect examples still exist.

Dawkins strolled around the environs of *Elymbos* meeting men who had worked on the railways of Madagascar, a dam at Aswan and further afield. Following the example of the Bents he walked down the valley to Diafani, though without mishap. He doesn't bother describing the village, but takes us immediately to Palatia where he sketched the church and medieval remains. And now something strange happens. Not to him, but to me. I was visiting Palatia with two men from the village. Using Notes from Karpathos as a guide we climbed up the southern promontory to the remains of the chapel of *Agios Nikolaos*. Following Dawkins we stumbled across two rock tombs. I stood alongside them reading Dawkins aloud as he described returning to the village:

The only good prehistoric object I was able to obtain
was a small black stone axe that I bought at *Elymbos*.
It was found in the island of Saria, near the site now
called *Ta Palatia*.

One of my companions was only half listening as he was
reading his grandfather's old notebook. The grandfather
was a prominent citizen of Olymbos and interested in antiquities. Translating into English he read aloud:

And then an Englishman came to the village and I
sold him a small black stone axe I had discovered at
Palatia.

And suddenly I was transported back into another century where Dawkins and the grandfather talked to one another once again and an axe was sold.

Robert Liddell (13 October 1908 - 23 July 1992) was a
shy and retiring man, an English literary critic, biographer,
novelist, travel writer and poet. From 1933 to 1938 he
worked at the Bodleian Library in Oxford. He lived briefly
in Athens before the Second World War, while working for
the British Council, before fleeing to Egypt where he ob-
tained work as a lecturer at the Universities of Cairo and
Alexandria. Lightly disguised, he appears in the novel *For-
tunes of War* by Olivier Manning. From 1953 to 1972 Liddell
was employed by the University of Athens, serving for part
of the time as head of the English Department. He travelled
extensively, but never returned to England. In June 1953
Liddell was in Rhodes waiting for a boat to leave for Karpathos. Recent travellers will understand the experience.
His craft was the fishing boat Acropolis; at first the captain
could not decide if he wanted to sail and then the har-
bourmaster would not allow them to leave. Eventually, after a 12 hour wait they sailed at 7 pm:

on a blue and primrose sea as the sun was setting.

Liddell had a rather sour, understated view of life; an electric light above his bed kept him him awake all night, though why he did not take the bulb out we shall never know. In the morning they arrived at Diafani:

a dull port, but the ride inland is magnificent....

He travelled by mule up to Olymbos:

at first the path was up a dry river bed, where olean-
ders were growing: later this narrowed into a deep
gorge, with pines growing from its rocky banks.....the
pines, bent double by the wind...evil and sinis-
ter...gave no shade worth having.

Reaching the top he tells us:

Olymbos was like turning a page in an early nine-
teenth-century travel book, and a ring of staring faces
in the cafe greeted my arrival and there was not even
any coffee to be had.

Liddell stayed with Papa Halkias who gave him two clean, upper rooms. The priest and his wife slept below but the priest ate upstairs with Liddell; the food: rice, soup, roast kid, fresh bread and a cucumber imported from Rho-des was brought through a trapdoor in the floor by the *pappadhia*, the priest's wife. Nothing seems to have pleased Liddell: he was not impressed with the food: describing the kid, which must have been free range and fresh, as:

all right, I daresay, if you like kid.

The next day his mood was no better as he visited:

the ugly hamlet of Avlona.

That night, walking through Olymbos with a young boy for a guide, he came across a rock where a young woman had committed suicide the previous Good Friday. As Liddell tells the story:

> In her white breeches she had sat on the edge, wailing for her dead father, dead some ten days before. Nobody knew her intent and nobody came to her rescue until, slithering forward, she fell and died. Father Halkias blessed the place with holy water otherwise nobody would pass the spot and the villagers expected the self-slayer to become a vampire. Instead she appeared in a dream to a schoolboy almost immediately after her death and told him:

> tell my son Minas not to cry; I'm all right.

Later Liddell saw Minas in the village:

> a gentle, sad, plain little boy.

Liddell wanted to ask more of Halkias but after a christening in Olymbos the *Papas* had to hurry off to Diafani as:

> Unfortunately someone has died at Diafani. I must bury him tonight; in weather like this he won't keep till tomorrow.

Clearly Liddell was experiencing a reality normally hidden from tourists. The seemingly casual attitude to death continues to this day:

> It's natural.

> I am repeatedly told.

Liddell often had groups of small children gathered around him. A woman passed and swore at one of them, a lad called Phillip. Liddell asked the boys why?

> Because he teases her son at school and calls him a bastard.

Which he is, said Phillip and a third boy Georgos chimed in:

She had him without a husband

before asking if there were bastards in England. Poor Liddell was now in a deep argument of relative morality. Clearly a liberal he argued with the boys that the father was as much at fault as the mother, but all the children would concede was:

Perhaps it's a little his fathers fault, but mostly his mother's.

After a few days in Olymbos, Liddell continued his journey, setting off south by mule, but he argued with the:

soft spoken, false and hypocritical muleteer.

And turned to the sea at the:

nasty little village of Spoa.

At the tiny port of Agios Nikolaos he caught a *caique* to Pigadia. Liddell consider Karpathos a grim place with unattractive people resembling a very lost tribe of Israel. He never came back. In the village they tell me:

Life is like a cucumber. Some like it, and some don't

Clearly Liddell didn't like it.

Eleni

Eleni is, as they say, quite a character. Widowed for a decade now and with a single son she has little money, but is nevertheless, a cheerful woman. Slightly bow-legged with bristly chin and a few randomly distributed teeth she laughs and smiles and carries out a one sided conversation with whoever walks past her *periptero*: the kiosk by the sea, where she sells paper handkerchiefs, disposable razors and other bits and pieces. For some time I have been collecting *toubres*, the brightly coloured, indigenous woven bags that are worn like a rucksack. They are not grand objects, but represent a recent history and are dear to me. Some of my collection belonged to the families of friends; one is nearly a hundred years old and a rich mixture of reds, mauves and lilac. Useful *toubres* are lined and one that I bought from an old lady has a lining made from the trousers of her grandson, my friend Iannis Sofoulis, though he wore the trousers long before we met.

It was an old *toubra* that attracted Eleni's attention, so old that even the patches have been patched. She came out of the *periptero* shaking her head and waving her arms and told me she would find me a new one. Trying to avoid complications I didn't take much notice of what she was telling me, just walked past nodding and smiling as she nodded and smiled at me. Night after night she said the same things and I continued, pretty much, to ignore her. Until one evening she dragged me into the kiosk and there was a brand new *toubra*. Well, not exactly brand new, the base material was hand woven by her grandmother from goats hairs, but Eleni had embroidered outlandish colours on the outside and there it was: for me: a *toubra.*

Now I understood what she had been saying. But what to do? Was it really for me? I had not asked for it: Eleni had just decided that I needed a new bag. Was it a present? Should I pay? How much? I did not want to upset this kind woman, did not want to offend local moral codes. Panic.

Eleni has a natural grace. She put the *toubra* on my back, smoothed it down, told me it looked good:

Should I pay?

Ah meh. Why not?

How much?

How much do you want to pay.

????????? Is 25 euros ok?

30 euros would make me happy.

So I had a new *toubra* unsuspected and unasked for, but mine. What is interesting is the number of comments it gets from the people of the village. Clearly these bags are part of their recent history and are carried in folk memory. They are pleased to see me wearing one, don't think I look a total idiot and make pleasant comments as if I have metamorphosed:

Orea toubras, esai Afaniotes, chorianos esai. Wonderful *toubra*s, you're from the village, one of us.

They insist that a *toubra* is used for carrying food and the food has to be: bread, olives and goats cheese. But strangely, for a centuries old design, my MacBook fits perfectly.

The Hirakis

There are several Hirakis brothers and one sister. They all have the same characteristics: they work hard, are honest, tough and strong. All were born in absolute poverty. Some were born in stables alongside sheep and cows, at least two were born in a cave. These are formidable people and I like to think we are friends. The two that I know best, Vassillis and his eldest brother Michalis, work together as builders and plasterers.

Their work rate is something to behold. They use a double sized wheelbarrow when plastering, mixing up around 50 kilo of plaster in a mixer, before flipping it onto the hot, dry walls. Ten minutes later they need another barrow load as they take it in turns; one smooths the wall while the other mixes the plaster.

Those of you who have been in the building trade would know what I mean by a two and a half bag cement mixer. Basically it is big and would fill two of these large wheelbarrows at one go. One day, while having coffee in Anna's I looked up to see Michalis lope past, pulling his mixer behind him. I would struggle to shift such a thing twenty metres at best. Michalis, strolling along in his nonchalant way, was taking it to the other end of the harbour. Years ago, when I first came to the village and did not know any better, I was fascinated by Michalis' massive forearms, his lop sided, heavy jawed face and his purposeful stride and I called him Popeye. The nickname stuck, but please don't tell him it was me who named him thus for he is a very strong man.

What I like about the family is that they are as intrigued by me as much as I am by them. They respect me because I write and used to teach in a university, but they treat me as an equal and make jokes about me. Michalis finds it funny that I read books:

Mia zoi kai diabases?

He shouts at me in the mornings:

One life and you read?

And he shakes his head in amazement:

Don't you know it all yet?

Nobody in this village has just one job: Vassillis is a restauranteur in the evening and a fireman at night and both brothers are shepherds. Shepherding is not an easy profession in a hot, dry, thorny, mountainous landscape. Vassillis has sheep on the high mountain above Avlona while Michali has goats on Saria. Shepherds keep dogs here, but cannot use them to fetch their *zoa*, animals, as the rocks and thorns would destroy their paws. Instead, wearing high boots, they chase after the sheep and goats themselves. I fancy I am fit, but a cliff or mountain slope that would take me more than an hour to climb takes Vassillis or Michaelis less than ten minutes to run up and they do not get out of breath. Coming down they use *glitses*, three metre long shepherds' crooks, with a large hook on one end and a wicked spike at the other. With *glitses* they and their women folk pole vault at lightning speed down mountain slopes, five or six metres at a time; no doubt this exercise contributes to their big shoulders and triangular forearms.

One soft, early autumn evening Vassilis and I were sharing a retsina as he told me about his brothers. Family ties are unbreakable here and big brothers are expected to look after their younger siblings. When Vassilis was fifteen years old, he was a big lad and strong, but no match for a man from another village: Iannis, a vicious bully, some twenty years older. Having served a term for murder, Iannis had recently been released from prison. The confrontation was in a small orchard near Tristomo: a wild and desolate place and lonely if you are going to take a beating and Vassillis was in trouble. He had his back to the sea as Iannis approached and scoured the mountains for his brother Michaelis, who was somewhere nearby. He climbed a tree to escape his assailant and as Iannis approached he screamed for help and screamed and screamed and screamed. There was the bark of a dog, a flash of white and suddenly Michaelis was coming down the mountain like a demented kayaker. He was not pole vaulting, but using the crook two handed: one end to the other: an awesome and terrifying sight.

Vassillis laughed gently as he recalled the scene:

Did Iannis run?

I asked. There is a pause and more laughter and he tells me:

He's still running.

I am a person of habit in the village: up early in the morning I have a simple breakfast before wandering out for a coffee prior to the arrival of the tourist boat. I try to write in the late morning and early afternoon and wait until the tourists have gone before descending the stairs from my house for a swim off the small beach in the village. Lately this regime takes me past Michaelis and Vassillis as they plaster a nearby house. Of course I am the subject of ribald remarks. I try to give as good as I get, but it is very strange to the brothers that a sensible person of my age goes swimming every day. They are strong and fit and have no need for aerobics or fitness regimes, so they shout at me in rustic fashion:

Alatines na myn halai? Do you put salt on it so it doesn't decay?

And they make rude gestures of sexual innuendo. I try to respond, but they are more adept than me and I am using a second language. One day Michaelis recited a *mantinada*. It was clearly about me and I was honoured. I asked Michaeli to tell me the *mantinada,* but his dialect is very heavy and I only understood a few words, so he wrote it down for me. I thanked him, but schooling is not his strong point and I could not read his writing. I asked Georgos to help, but he could not read the *mantinada* either. Nothing is easy in this village and you have to be cunning. Georgos is cunning. He didn't want to embarrass Michaelis for having bad handwriting, so he explained that the wind had blown the *mantinada* away and could Michaelis write it again. At first Michaelis refused, walking away with his loaded wheelbarrow, pretending he had forgotten. This big, strong, hard man, Popeye, was shy and self-conscious at what he had done. Eventually, with help from Vassilis we got it down. I can no more translate *mantinades* into English than I can translate Shakespeare sonnets into Classical Greek. But....

Agapise to topo mas me ola ta ensticta tou

progamoitises ekdromes kratas kai to toubra tou

He loves our place with all his instinct
takes daily walks clutching his *toubra*

A simple verse, it pins me precisely. One day I will hear it sung at a *glendi* and everyone will laugh.

Two Sisters

They are two sisters living alone on a triangular plateau south of the village. I will not reveal their location: they should not be disturbed. On two sides of the plateau there are mountains, on the third is a cliff tumbling to the sea. The sisters live in a small *stavlos*, a single roomed dwelling of stone and cement with a soil and cement roof held up by untrimmed rafters. They sleep on the floor, hidden away in a dark room with a small fireplace. They have no electricity, no toilet, no running water. The remains of a small wind generator can be seen on the roof: at one time it provided a dim light, but the blades were swept away in a storm so now the sisters adopt the old method: they arise with the sun and sleep when it sets. The nearest water is a spring one kilometre away. Daily they make the trek to fetch a *biton* of eighteen litres of water, for them and their livestock. They keep goats: a flock of around forty, and they have cats and dogs. One of the dogs has three legs. The ladies explain the poor animal disappeared for four days and when found it had wire wrapped round its leg and the leg was septic so they amputated. The goats and the dogs are well cared for.

We are here to look at the birds and check on the wild life. We are not here to visit the women, but they are fascinating company and pleased to talk, so we stay with them awhile. We are given a plate of *drilla*: the thick, white savoury that tastes of butter and cream cheese. We sit on tiny stools, out of the sun, balancing fat slices of bread on our knees. The sisters were born in the mid nineteen thirties, they are strong and healthy, though one seems to be blind in one eye. Conversation is difficult as their dialect is thick, but it is possible to get a rough idea of their life. I ask if they can read and am told they never went to school; they worked in the fields from the age of three: chasing birds and moving the goats up the mountainsides away from the crops.

They remember the Italians coming at the beginning of the war (which they think was around 1937) and, in concert with other farmers, hiding livestock and grain from the German occupiers. They have relatives in the village and can walk there in three hours unless, they tell me, they have a heavy load to carry, in which case it is four. Someone gave them a mobile phone with big buttons but, without electricity, the battery is flat and we have no charger in the car. A child has written one telephone number in large figures on a scrap of paper and there is a child's picture of a house, with smoke coming from the chimney and two stick ladies outside. We promise to call the number when in the village and order, fruit and flour, matches and cakes. They love cakes.

Sitting with them I am not in this century, nor the last, or the one before that. The conversation has a medieval ring to it: what they see is what they know. I ask about the land in front of us and receive a treatise on ownership and family ties. Pointing to each field and corner in turn they reveal a magnificent oral knowledge of kinship and ownership: this small field belongs to Iannis L, who was married to Sophi whose son Georgos went to America for forty years and his grandchildren came back last summer. That one was our mother's and she left it to our brother who died last year, so now it is divided between his two daughters. The stony field over there belongs to Maria H who married the shepherd from Spoa. She inherited it from our aunt who died in the war and she is getting old now so her daughter Marina will get it. And on and on. I ask about the bird life. Of course there are eagles here and *mavropetritis*, Eleanora's falcons, and one time a pelican arrived. The pelican must have been quite a sight trundling over the mountains to this 400 metre high plateau. In those days there was a pond and there must have been frogs and salamanders and other amphibia, but the water table lowers by twenty centimetres a year and the pond is now intermittent. It is late spring on the day of our visit and the fields are full of larks and other passerines. Their song mixes with the soft gargle of bee eaters as they whiz over the high stone walls surrounding the rocky fields. From time to time the chuckle of *perdikes,* partridges, trickles down the mountainside.

The sisters are happy to have company; laughing and pointing as they lead us to a small hut a hundred metres away. Here they make cheese. Inside we see forty or more moulds of cheese and along the edge of the roof another twenty, maturing in the sun. They chose one for us and tell me to soak it in salt water for a day and then it will be ready. They force me to eat more *drilla* and when I try to resist one of them tells me:

Tha sou cammo ena ios, I will make you my son

and laughs when I don't understand and tells me it is because she speaks Byzantian and has old thoughts.

We are here to look for eagles so we leave them for a while and take the steep path opposite. As we climb we can hear the sisters talking to their goats, each with its own name, and we see the three legged dog hopping about and barking. It is hot in the morning sun and from the ridge we see the boundaries of their life. Except for the daily trek for water and the occasional visit to the village, their world is five hundred metres in diameter, 'though they don't seem restricted by their geography, nor indeed their history.

These are tough women, but open and friendly to strangers, bright and cheerful and full of energy. They have nephews and nieces and a cousin or two and clearly don't feel abandoned.

We complete our survey of the area: no eagles, no buzzards, but plenty of Eleanora's above and around us which is a pleasant surprise as these are rare birds and must nest on a previously unrecorded colony on the seaward side of the mountain on the west side of the island. We return to the plateau, pick up our cheese and find the sisters have written a list of shopping. The word cakes is underlined twice. As we go to the car the sister with one eye shouts thank you for coming and say hello to....and she struggles for the word, say hello to....*To Cosmos.*

To Cosmos means cosmos, the world, universe, earth, realm....everything.

Say hello to *To Cosmos* puts their life in context.

Some things do not exist

The super rich are uncouth, inconsiderate, insensitive, lack taste and have no love for life. I know this because they have yachts: not the sleek yachts that face rough seas with sails and engines, not the old wooden yachts, smelling of oil and tar, but new, massive, ugly yachts driven by oil guzzling diesel engines. As much as three stories high and one hundred metres long, they can be black, white and god forgive, gold. They come with gourmet chefs, high-class whores, jacuzzis, jet-skis, speedboats and several bars. They are gross, soulless, floating 7 star hotels that waste the planet to satisfy the egos of inadequate men. Without any consideration for the environment these people proceed to plonk their ugly boats in the middle of some of the most beautiful spots in the world. They pollute the scenery.

Steno is special. Narrow at the eastern end (*steno* means narrow), it widens westwards to a one kilometre natural amphitheater. Never still, rarely calm, it can be dangerous in a small boat, but at dusk in the late autumn it has peace and unsurpassed majesty. I have seen Monk seals there, eagles gathering before they head south to Africa, marsh harriers and many kinds of heron. In thirty years I have seen it calm one time only. Two hours later came a massive storm, terrifying in its intensity. There is always a current at Steno. It changes direction twice a day; if the wind and the current move in the same direction the water surface moves along at ten knots an hour making a boat hard to control; if the current moves against the wind, waves pile up, sometimes two metres high and the captains of small boats get wet. I like to fish in Steno: depending on the year and the time of day it is possible to catch *palamida* and tuna fish, barracuda and *kinigos*. These days the lure I pull has ten hooks and if I hit a shoal, can catch four or more fish at a time. Then I have to work hard to pull the line in while I steer the boat at the right speed, but in a curve so the fish come over the side. Meanwhile I try to avoid the rocks and shallows. As the line comes into the boat I must put the hooks to one side and hope they do not catch in the spools of nylon; if the hook has a fish I must first get it into the boat and then take it off the hook without getting the hook in my hands or feet, or worse still, my eyes. So far I have been lucky: I have scars on my hands and holes in my jeans, but the rest of me is intact: more, or less. *Kinigos* is the best fish to catch: once in the boat they tend to fall off the hook and die fast, without causing chaos. They are also good to eat. Tuna are another matter. Even a two kilo tuna is a dangerous fish: to pull it in you have to wrap the line around your hand: this hurts and could be dangerous. Imagine it is a ten kilo fish, stronger than a pit bull fighting for its life, imagine the pain as the blood to the fingers is cut off. Alongside the boat I use a gaff to bring tuna over the side and into the boat. A big fish can create mayhem as it thrashes around close to my bare feet, perhaps with the gaff in its side and with several hooks in its mouth. Somehow I must take the creature and bash it on the head with something heavy. When it is still I make a cut at the back of its head to let out the blood. Only then does fear subside and triumph takes over. If you think this is cruel, stop eating tuna.

Returning one evening from a long day's dive on the northeast side of Saria, Georgos and I were trolling a single lure, looking for barracuda. We know where they gather and the light was going, so we had high hopes. We turned west into Steno and saw the sun setting between the islands: a flame of red, orange, yellow and gold. Inside the straits we turned north to be confronted suddenly by a towering, black, ugly yacht anchored off Iaplo. We carried on fishing. We turned and travelled down the starboard side of the ship, under the bow, past the anchor chain, along the port side, under the stern and away again towards Alona. There was no sign of life on this repulsive mass: no sound and no lights. The myriad of windows and portholes were of course tinted to stop anyone seeing inside, but we did not want to look, we just carried on our way. We did not catch anything as we circumnavigated the monster and having no wish to provide entertainment for its passengers, I was glad. Neither Georgos nor I said anything and to this day neither of us have mentioned the black yacht. Sometimes it is the only way.

Frogs

Visitors to the village make the assumption that it acts as some kind of co-operative, with everybody helping one another. They are mistaken. This is a small village with a handful of families and each person feels allegiance first and foremost to their family. After that, maybe, comes the village. They will help their family and they will help strangers and are wonderful to me, but co-operation is not a byword here. The only exception is at sea where, if you have a problem, villagers rush to your assistance. Until recently life here was very difficult: villagers nearly starved to death and had to work incredibly hard to survive: families competed with one another for limited resources. Memories of those times do not fade easily and except when faced with a common enemy, such as in wartime, the village has never developed a mechanism for mutual support. To this day nobody will work for another family in the village: they work for themselves, or they migrate.

And now we come to the frogs. Not any frogs, but special frogs: the Karpathos Frog (*Pelophylax Cerigensis*) is in the *Ranidae* family and is unique to the island. A cute little creature, there are only a few hundred left and we are doing our best to save them. The Greek government and the European Community provide funds for the endeavour and we are making progress in protecting them. A long time before this support, there was much talk in the village about these animals. One day leaflets appeared: distributed on restaurant tables and pinned to telegraph poles. With the heading - Save the Frogs- the leaflets explained there was a job opportunity for a person who could demonstrate they were hard working and cared for frogs. The pay was good and the conditions were generous and all the applicant had to do was present themselves the next Monday morning at the office in Pigadia. The people here are smart, they realised the fewer applicants there were the better chance they had of getting the job. So the leaflets disappeared. First they went from the tables, then they were torn from the telegraph poles and disappeared into pockets. Soon, all that remained of these public offers of career enhancement were a few coloured pins and shreds of paper flapping in the breeze. And nobody said a word.

Monday morning saw several men on the little shopping boat going south to Pigadia. They did not, as normal, sit and gossip in the cabin, instead they strolled around on deck, staring out to sea, avoiding one another's inquisitive glances. On arrival at the port they left the boat hurriedly, fanning out in different directions, trying to keep an eye on their competitors. The leaflet had not given the name or address of the office. This was no major obstacle as there are only a handful of offices in the town. All the applicants had to do was go from one office to another and show their copy of the leaflet. Of course they had to do this without leading their fellow villagers to the office concerned. All day a game of hide and seek continued as men moved in and out of offices, asked questions while discretely showing a crunched up leaflet and left. By the end of the day they were being laughed at in office after office and it gradually dawned they had been fooled: there was no office, there was no job: the leaflet was a spoof. Shamefaced, but still avoiding one another, they returned to the village muttering revenge on the perpetrator of the hoax. To this day, they do not know who it was, and I am not telling.

The rapid extinction of species is a serious and worsening problem and if well known and sympathetic animals like the snow leopard, or the Indian tiger face oblivion how can we possibly save the less glamorous creatures? *Pelophylax Cerigensis* are found nowhere else in the world but this island. Years ago they were many of them and they were found in several locations. Then came forest fires and hotels and cars and restaurants that needed to be washed every day, so the water table got lower and there are fewer frogs.

Like most wild creatures in this area they are benign, they do not make a fuss when approached and seem quite happy to be picked up. In the UK frogs lay eggs in the spring, subsequently tadpoles grow and mature over the summer until, by autumn, they have become small frogs. On the island this process appears to be different and varies according to the water supply. If there is little winter rain and the summer is long the mature frogs bury themselves deep in mud and hibernate. Eggs are laid whenever there is water and tadpoles appear to take more than one summer to develop.

If I sound vague it is because nobody seems to have studied these animals. Talking to the old men in the *cafeneion* at night, they ask me why I am interested in these humble creatures and what use they are to mankind. I explain about incurable diseases and the possibility of finding useful medicines exuded by these frogs. They look at me, heads on one side, seemingly unconvinced: as well they should be, for I have invented the fable. I cannot explain why these little animals are important for the quality of life. But I know they are. We have been brought up to believe that the world is teeming with creatures, but it is not. Because of man there are plenty of gulls, cats, rats and cockroaches. But most of the sea is barren and without fish, all the lions in the world could fit into one medium sized football stadium and all the *pelophylax cerigensis* could be carried in one bucket. And this frightens me.

Mantinades

There are many facets of life in the village described by outsiders as traditional; the food, women's clothes, the music, the inheritance laws, arranged marriages, *mantinades* and the inventive use of language. To study them separately, as some academics do, is to miss the point: village life is woven together to form a living cultural palimpsest. *Mantinades* are rhyming couplets of fifteen syllables each, sometimes beautiful, often humorous or vicious and intended to hurt, they reflect the obsessions of the age and the society which gave birth to them, but in order to appreciate their subtlety you must understand village life.

Most marriages in the village are arranged, not forced, but arranged. In a small village with a limited gene pool it makes sense not to marry close relatives and thus the choice for young people from within the village is limited. The diaspora adds variety, but requires a knowledge of family structure and relationships stretching back generations. Here, old ladies come into play. *Giagiades,* grandmothers, can remember who emigrated where and who married who, three or four generations back, and thus who is a suitable match, even if they have never set foot in the village. Grandmothers talk to one another, arrange introductions, make persuasive noises and negotiate the dowry or bride price. A side effect of this activity is that old ladies in the village are well respected by their grandchildren. Of course, young people can act independently and if the family does not approve, there is an alternative and one, which, in the age of romantic love, is becoming more prevalent. A man can become *kleftis* and steal his bride. The way it is done is for the couple to go away and telephone the bride's parents to say; we want to get married, we would like your support, but if not we are staying in a hotel and..... Most parents dote on their daughters and the act of the thief is usually sanctified by parental approval.

It was not always like this. A semi-literate, unbalanced woman did not approve of her son's choice and forbade the marriage. The son took his love to Pigadia, defied his mother and married the girl. To smooth the way to a better relationship, the new bride wrote to her mother-in-law to say she would like to be friends. The mother could have compromised, been forgiving, written a polite but distant letter. Instead she responded with a *mantinada*, almost Shakespearean in impact.

> *Agnosti Fountaliena pou nacheis tou kamo mou grafe mou*
> *Se parakalw pou kames ton yio mou?*

> Unknown Fontaliena who wishes me well
> Tell me, what have you done with my son?

One can imagine the pain this rhyme caused at the time and villagers still talk about it five decades after the event. Another *mantinada* from that time expresses the humour of courtship. To understand it you need to know the names of the different winds and their direction. Starting from the north and moving clockwise we have; *tramountana* (N), *graigos, lebantes* (E), *sorokos, ostria* (S), *garmpis, mpounentis* (W) and *maistros* (NW).

A girl, Erniw, was being courted by Iannis Kipraio, a man whose eyes were crossed. Her mother, being opposed to the marriage, ridiculed the poor man by drawing attention to his affliction:

Ti na ton itheles, Erniw ton Iannis tou Kipraio
Apou thwron ta matia tou ostria, garmpis kai graigos

What do you want Erniw with Iannis Kipraio
Who has eyes that *are ostria, garmpis and graigos?*

Another, written by a man shortly before he died, expressed happiness and joy. He was full of life and today when the men feel good they sing his song:

Den xero an einai sti zwi kai echw akoma tratos
Gia afto tha pino kai tha trw na paw skia chortatos

I do not know if my life has more time
So I drink and I eat to be a satisfied ghost

Perhaps the funniest *mantinada* was written by a man who had gone out for a meal in his friend's restaurant. The restauranteur had been a shepherd with a flock at Arki on Saria and did not really like his new life. So preoccupied was he that he forgot he had a customer and thinking the restaurant was empty, absent minded locked up and went home. The customer managed to let himself out. Before he did so he scribbled:

Den eisai esi yia to magazi ute pelateia
Mono na pais sto Arki na kyniges arnia

You are not for clientele or for shops
Only to go to Arki to chase your flocks

I am no poet and my translations are rough and ready. The originals, produced by working men and women with little or no education can be very clever and very beautiful. There are hundreds of *mantinades* in general use and each birth, death or festival brings more. Academics collect them to pin down like butterflies in collections. But butterflies are best seen when wild and free and blown by the wind and *mantinades* are best heard round a table loaded with whisky or retsina and sung in a collective expression of sadness or joy.

Michalidi-Little Michalis

Michalis is a gentleman, one of the old kind, perhaps the last of the old kind. Small and slim, almost dainty, with hands held behind a ramrod straight back he prowls the village saying hello to a lady here, a small child or tourist over there. Michalis wears spectacles and a captain's hat, but neither conceals his button-bright eyes, native intelligence or easy smile. The man loves to gossip, loves to tell stories of the old times and is the source of many of my tales, so it was to him I turned to solve a problem. I wanted to know about a man called Fournourouthanos, Oven-Nostrils. I came across the name some time ago while researching *American Ikaros*, the biography of Kevin Andrews and realised that decades before I had met Fournourouthanos. He was about the same age as Michalis, but died a few years ago. I knew he had a massive appetite, was immensely strong, but not very bright: though nobody told him to his face, and would bet on anything. His nickname arose from having extraordinarily large nostrils.

What I did not expect when I asked if he knew this strange sounding man was Michalis' reaction. Like a cartoon character who has lost control, Michalis erupted with fury. He started to shout and leapt into the air so high his feet seemed further off the ground than his hands. I didn't know what to say or what to do and was even more confused when I realised Michalis was repeating a *mantinada*. When he calmed down I got him to write out the *mantinada* and with the help of others a story emerged.

It was soon after the end of the Second World War, food was scarce and Michalis had a big family to feed. There was a famine: in parts of Greece people were dying of starvation and life was very hard. Michalis had a favourite fig tree on his wife's land in Saria, the stock coming originally from Halki, an island to the north. One day in the autumn he went with his wife to collect figs. It was hot as they struggled through the stony, thorny, dry landscape to their tree. As they got close they saw movement. Fournourouthanos! He was up in the tree and had eaten half the figs. Furiously Michalis chased the much larger intruder away. When he returned to the ravaged tree his wife had composed the following;

Sikia mou charkihki ta sika fourtomeni

Irthen o Fournourouthounos kai tromazei caimanei

My fig tree from Halki was full of figs

Along came Fournourouthanos and now it's twigs

Michalis is a kind and generous man always willing to share what he has or lend a hand. For his anger to last 60 years tells us about the times he lived through and the *mantinada* carries that message.

A seat in the *Cafeneion*

I go to the *cafeneion* twice a day and like to sit outside in the small *avli* and catch the news of the day. In the morning I take a coffee, *Hellenico sketo,* without sugar. Of course I don't have to explain what I want as Anna knows my taste: all I do is make a gesture and in my turn will be served a small, strong, bitter, Greek (initially Turkish) coffee.

If I am lucky I will be left in peace and my mind will drift as the other old men argue about the economy, or Obama, Iraq or Libya, or some other matter in which, of course, they are expert. Then I can look at the panorama, surely the best in Greece, of the sea, sky and mountains. Consider the sea. Try to imagine a blank page or maybe a screen. Make it grey. Measure one third from the bottom and draw a line across. Make the line dip a fraction at each edge. That will do for the horizon. Now decide on the colour of the sky. Any schoolchild will tell you that the sky is blue. Any schoolchild will tell you that the sea is blue. Ask them if it is the same blue. No. Ask them if the sea is black and white and grey, silver and green. Yes. Well, a little bit. Examine the questions closer. Ask a three or four year old to paint the sky. They will use any colour they want. Ask a six year old. The sky is blue. They believe it is blue because they are told it is blue. It is not. Look at the sea again, look at the sky. Close your eyes. What is the colour now? All of the above and yellow and gold, sometimes even red or purple and it is in lumps and heaps, thick like oil painting in whirls and flurries, or flat in a subtle blend like a wash on a water-colour. And in one minute it will be different so you have to start again.

I have a favourite seat in the evenings and use what cunning I have to make it mine. Another small gesture and an *ouzo* arrives with olives or cucumber, dry bread or salt fish. I look north across the half-moon bay of the village I hear the waves and the murmur of women as they gossip in the dark. Sometimes in late spring, or in the autumn when it is cool or a little damp there is, for a millisecond, an unbearable feeling of deep nostalgia. For a brief, poignant moment I am able to hold the sadness, but a boat's engine kicks into life or an argument starts among the men playing cards inside the *cafeneion* and the moment is gone. I look again at the mountains and the sea and the sky. By now the sun has gone down and the sky is a pale tint of blue, light behind the mountains, darker at the peaks. Sparkling gold stars are scattered about in the gloaming and the moon rises to light up the mountainside until it shines white against the darkling sky and silver sea. As the moon rises the mountains lighten and the sea shines and the sky blackens and more stars are seen, now silver in their constellations. Kevin Andrews used to sit in the same place with the same thoughts. Perhaps he found some peace and could relax for once amid the turmoil of his life. Quiet and calm with the soft moan of the sea, these moments can only be experienced by those who are truly alone.

Every Corner has a Story

The *Anixis* restaurant serves good, home cooked, village food. The lady of the house, Eleni does the cooking while Vassillis, her husband, is a shepherd with flocks on the mountains to the north of the village. The restaurant has a history. Vassillis tells me it is the site of the first *cafeneion* in the village and the old house that forms one side of the *avli* was one of the first in the village. A century ago it was owned by a sea captain named Kostas Protopapas who was the grandfather of the mother of Eleni. His boat was, the Olga, a *maounas* driven by oars and sail. He shipped out sheep and goats in those days and imported rice and grain. Gradually Kostas became an *emporevma* or merchant and the Anixis became a *mpakalis*, a Turkish word for grocery store.

There was no road down from *to chorio* in those days, only footpaths and a donkey track. The men came down with their donkeys to the beach to wait for the Olga to arrive and while they waited they were served coffee in the store and hung around exchanging news and gossip and flirting with the local girls. My friend Minas Prearis, in his younger days a village Romeo, used to volunteer to come down from *to chorio* in order to court his wife. When a bakery and sweet shop opened in Pigadia, Kostas imported cakes and sweet things and sold them along with coffee.

As time passed Anna's *cafeneion* opened, the Olga was replaced by boats with engines and the little mole in Diafani was constructed to accommodate the modern craft; *karaboskara* and *caiquia*. In the seventies the Anixis became what was known as the OTE. There were no telephones in private houses in those days and you came to the OTE to make telephone calls to the outside world or to send telegrams. The women of the family worked the exchange and commented on what you were saying. Nothing was secret and every conversation you had and every telegram you dictated was shared with the villagers who had no shame in commenting on your news. Telegrams were expensive in those days and there is the story of an old captain who arrived here and wanted to telegram his wife:

ARRIVED SAFELY CALM SEAS

he wrote and was told it would be 5 drachmes per word for a total of 20 drachmes.

He asked for the form back and rewrote the telegram:

ARRIVEDSAFELYCALMSEAS

and got away with paying 5 drachmes.

OTE soon put a stop to this artifice.

While Eleni is clearly the boss, Vassillis is very proud of the restaurant and loves to deal with the customers in a halting mixture of broken tongues. When they ask where the sheep comes from he shows off by pointing to this mountain slope or that valley. Sometimes his enthusiasm is too strong: a Parisian family were finishing their stew. They enjoyed what they ate:

Lovely lamb

the mother commented. Vassillis was pleased and told them:

Yes, I just killed it.

They looked a bit surprised, but were back the next night.

In the autumn, when the tourists have gone, the streets are dark and it is easy to for the women to come and go without being noticed, I love to sit in the Anixis while Eleni embroiders her daughter's trousseau and listen to the gossip. A figure might slip past in the shadows: tall, slim, dark, beautiful; black blouse, black skirt, black boots, she is an actor from a perfectly crafted film by Theodoros Angelopoulos, or she is Evangeleia, going to the shop and it is time for me to drain my glass and go to bed.

How are you Feeling?

For many years I wanted to own a house in the village. I needed some permanence here. It was a vain wish since they only sell property to family members. As I grew to understand more about the people I accepted their view; a mixture of financial acuity and sentimentality. It is a shame, I was once told, to have a stranger live in the house where your grandparents lived. Perversely they have no compunction about knocking down their grandparent's houses and building a new one, so the village is continually renewing and expanding and at least half the young men here follow one building trade or another.

It took some time before I came up with a plan to overcome the reluctance to sell. There are many empty houses in the village, owned by families in Rhodes, or Athens, Canada or America. Some have been empty for more than a generation. I didn't care about property speculation, I just wanted security of tenure, so why not rent one of these places and fix it up with a shower and electricity and when I died the house would go back to the family? I polished my plan, walked up and down the little alleys, up by the old church and down around the new. Even though it is a small village it is known by its districts. There is *Himonico*, winter, because the sun arrives late in the year and late in the day, *Parapotami*, by the river, *Vounara*, big mountain, *Plakakia*, the central 'square' and *Kamara*, by the big cave on the north side. I decided where I wanted to live, asked about families and focused upon a house that needed electricity and an inside toilet, but had a view of the sea. I have many friends in the village and one of them was Nikos, Mr Bow Wave, with a magnificent belly, wispy white hair and a wicked grin. A cynical man in his eighties he dedicated himself to pricking my pomposity and undermining my naivety. Noticing that my friend Georgos spends more time in my boat than I do, he once asked:

Who gets the boat?

And when I didn't understand. He spelled it out:

When you die, who gets the boat?

Hurtful and direct, but a good question. I was fascinated by Nikos; he lived many years in the far North of Canada, spoke Inuit and thought he was the first Greek at the North Pole. He spoke good English, so, over a coffee, I took my proposition to him:

How would it be if I took over a house, spent money to do it up, pay some rent and when I die it goes back to the family?

Nikos looked at me carefully, formed the question and asked directly:

How old are you?

Before I understood he was setting me up, I told him. A pause and with immaculate timing:

And how are you feeling?

I looked at him, saw the quizzical look and the hint of a grin. My self-importance was deflated as I laughed with him and gave up the dream of ex-patriot home ownership and rented a house instead. It is small, new, architecturally designed and built by friends of mine. My living room gives a view over the sea from one window, while from the other I see the mountains. In my bedroom I can hear the waves.

The house is built into the living rock below ground level, so it is cool in the summer and snug in the winter. From my balcony I see Bonnelli's eagles, ravens, bee eaters, Eleanora's falcons, kestrels and once a year an osprey or two. In the autumn blue rock thrush sit outside my veranda and compete for territory: the winner being the bird with the loudest song. Surrounded by old ladies who bake me bread I am without encumbrance and happy to be here. But I miss Nikos. A year ago he died without fuss and now there is an empty seat outside the *cafeneion*.

Weddings

Weddings in the village, are happy, vibrant affairs with music and dance, food, drink and gunfire. There are rarely less than 100 guests; one wedding I went to had so many guests that even the biggest hall in the village could not hold them all: the whole village was there and the wedding feast had to be held over two sittings of more than 500 each.

The wedding day starts in two houses, the bride in hers, the groom in his. The houses may be in separate villages but the pattern is the same. From early in the day the bride is bedecked and beautified as flowers arrive, hair is done and no matter how hot the weather, traditional clothes are worn. Much the same happens in the grooms house, except that drinking starts early or continues from the night before. As the day goes by visitors arrive and comment on the beauty of the bride and how handsome is the groom, presents are left and tears are shed while the two houses become crowded, actually overcrowded, and family and friends spill out onto the streets.

The wedding of a close friend, Dinos, was a confusing affair for this *romaios*, foreigner (you can see how old is the word). Until a few hours before the ceremony we did not know which church was going to be used in which village, what time the wedding would be and who would be the priest. When told we set off in our finery to the appropriate house. As a friend of the groom I went to his mother's house. This family are Sariatese, people of Saria: they have land and houses there, olive trees, goats and sheep. The house was crowded and every member of the family fulfilling a set role; some poured drinks, others passed around titbits, one brother paid for the beer, another the whisky. An uncle told me:

My job is to get you drunk.

When I arrived the mother of the groom pinned an embroidered handkerchief to my chest as a souvenir and to show my status, while his father pinned money onto musicians who would sing and play *mantinades*. The *meraklis* merited a 100 euro note, the others 50 euro each. Tension mounted as the agreed time to go to the church approached and mounted further as the hour passed. The mother, grandmother and brother of the groom sang *mantinades* praising his looks and demeanour. They sang how much they would miss him and, with tongue in cheek, asked him to reconsider the marriage and stay at home. The atmosphere was happy and sad, melancholic and joyful. Anastasia, the grandmother, over eighty with bright, blue eyes sang an extended ballad, tears running down her face. She recalled Dinos when he was young and opened her heart to tell us how much she would miss him:

Please don't go,

she sang:

please don't go.

And gave many reasons why he should stay: he was too young, he would find a better woman, he is needed at home:

Come again, once more into the mountains with the goats and sleep under the stars in the clean, salt air.

The ballad, composed over the previous weeks, was half in fun, half serious, traditional, but with the unique bite of this family and these people. Next, the mother tried to sing, but was overcome with emotion and had to give up. The whisky flowed and the tears too, as his brother, uncles and aunts came to kiss the groom and wish him well. All the time the music played and the tension mounted until the *meraklis*, the village postman, upped the decibels, changed the tempo and headed for the door. Suddenly we were under the night sky, parading through cool, dark, narrow alleyway singing joyful songs. When we arrived at the bride's house the doors and windows were open and we could see the house crammed with her friends and family. Now they were singing she should not go: the groom was not good enough for her and she should wait and find a better looking man with more money. Soon there were two choruses;

Inside:

Don't go. Stay with us, find a better man...

Outside:

Come with us, the dowry is good, you can live in Rhodes and Athens, have babies...

Suddenly the bride's party burst out into the alley and we were dancing and singing and there were tears and laughter as we made our way down the hill to the church. More songs outside the church and, because it is *to chorio* and there is always a fight, an argument broke out as to whether to have more songs or go inside. Papa Iannis restored peace by opening the double doors and we flooded into the church and went to our places: men on the right, women on the left, leaving the bride and groom, best man and bridesmaids alone at the front of the nave.

The service was simple and moving: Pappa Iannis blessed the bride and groom and sang ancient prayers. To recognise the presence of the holy trinity he led the couple three times round a ceremonial table bedecked with white flowers. They made vows to one another and to God and

the priest placed rings on the right hand of the bride and of
the groom. By now they were kneeling and wearing white
crowns tied together with long white ribbon. Pappa Iannis
exchanged the crowns three times, one to the other while
incanting words of goodness and joy as he beamed at the
congregation. The couple stood and kissed, friends and
family rushed forward to offer their congratulations and
good wishes and that was the end. Except for one inexplicable act. All the men got to beat the groom. We queued up
and took it in turns to pound the poor man on his back.
Dinos is a big man, all the men in his family are big and
they are tough and they laughed as the blows rained down.
Dinos stood his ground and flinched once only, when
pummelled by his brother, but that is another story. Then
off to dine on goat and rice and drink and dance through
the night and drink and drink: beer and retsina and whisky,
whisky, whisky. I left as the sky lightened above the sea on
the eastern horizon. I could hear voices floating over the
village in the morning breeze. They sounded drunk, but
maybe it was me.

Another, much grander wedding contained the same
drama, but on a larger scale. Three days before the day a
charming, unique little ceremony took place. Evangeleia is
smart and beautiful, very kind and like her father, a musician. Her family is central to village life and as the community is small she is constrained in her actions. Like many
young girls she occasionally lived away from home, in Rhodes and in that most dangerous of places: Crete. Some of
her Cretan friends came over on the ferry boat and one
night Evangaleia and a Cretan beauty sat and shared wine
and sang songs to one another. A simple act, but one that
could not occur in the West. Tensions mounted in the village as the wedding day approached and I awaited my in-
vite, but Evangeleia told me:

There are no invites, you just come.

And I did, and so did everyone else. It was impossible to get into the bride's house or even into the courtyard: there were too many family and friends, so I waited the other side of the street. And waited and waited as uncles and aunts, nephews and nieces, comrades and neighbours fought their way in and fought their way out. It was a hot August day and I was concerned as the bride appeared, beautiful, but very pale in the heavy, hot *kavai*, weighed down with bandoliers of gold coins. A smile for me, a faint kiss, then she was in the car and off, followed by dozens of cars and pick up trucks, up into the hills towards *to chorio*. I followed in the motorcade with hundreds of people laughing and crying, shouting and singing *mantinades* to the sound of bagpipes lutes and *lyras*.

In Olymbos there was mayhem: the streets thronged with people dancing and singing to centuries old music, while wild youths fired rifles and handguns from rooftops. It was impossible to get anywhere near the house of Georgos, the groom, but there were many rumours about his condition. He had been drinking with the boys from early morning, maybe from early evening the day before and he was, shall we say, mellow. I wanted to take photographs and younger friends helped me move from rooftop to rooftop and jump from hidden landings into hidden ally ways, across and through abandoned and occupied homes. Later, I found I had forgotten to put a film in my camera.

Suddenly a commotion; the groom is out of the house, dishevelled, but surrounded by friends and family he moves more or less under his own steam. The gunfire is deafening, there are thunder-flashes too, distress signals and rockets. Michaelis, the bride's father passes by singing and crying. He hugs me and kisses me full on the lips and is gone. His moustache tastes of whisky. I reach the church, this time with a loaded camera and climb high on a nearby roof so I see the bride's group converge with that of the groom as they ascend the steps to the church square. This is an important wedding: two good families united, a symbol of hope for the village, a merry madness in the air. It is impossible to enter the church, but I catch a glimpse of a pale, young Madonna and the groom valiantly supported by his friends. The ceremony lasts a long time and then the bells ring and they are out again in the hot, bright, August sunlight. I am swept along by happy villagers as shotguns fire and the village fills with red smoke. Someone grabs me and pulls me into a cool place and places a bottle of cold beer, *brasini*, green, (so Heineken), in my hand. I am exhausted.

The bars are jam packed and the alcohol flows, sometimes literally, down steps and alleys. Crowds stream past: some are going to the wedding feast, others are helped on their way home. Groups of musicians appear surrounded by dancers. I find my way to the *megaron*, a handkerchief is pinned to me, but I do not go inside: it is too crowded. A village united is laughing, smiling and rejoicing; food whizzes down tables, caps are flipped off bottles, toasts are made and music is played. It is hot. At one end of the hall, serene and beautiful, sits Evangelia. Alongside, with half closed eyes and beatific smile, her new husband, Georgos:

Goodnight, God bless.

I mutter, but nobody is listening as I fade away into the night.

Perfectly All Right

There are rules at sea: ways to behave. Everybody knows that sail gives way to steam, 'though if you have a 10 metre yacht I would advise you not to sail towards a 100,000 ton tanker coming your way. Here in the islands we have our own rules. If someone needs help at sea, there is no alternative: you give them help. If you find something interesting at sea it is yours, no matter who it belonged to before; find something on the beach and you leave it alone. And when you anchor your boat be careful where you lay your anchor and don't bump into other boats. I have followed and transgressed each of these rules: rescued boats when their engines have faltered and in turn been rescued myself. I find many good things in the sea; they adorn my house and my boat. I am not a fantastic boatman, but I have learned to anchor properly and I rarely bump into other craft.

My favourite trip, on a calm day, is to go north to Palatia. I have done this many times and can close my eyes and visualise the whole journey: slip the anchor, leave the port, slide past the rocks, tuck in under the cliffs to keep out of the wind, mind the reef, round the cape at Vananda, head into the wind, slow and turn again, so the wind is *prima*, coming over my shoulder. Keep going out past the next reef and then north again. The wind coming down the valley will turn and help me on my way. There are few sunken rocks to fear now: if I stay 30 metres out I will have no problem. Now to Kalamnia, a long, stony beach with two caves: good places to cool off on a hot day. Further north is

a magnificent tumble of rocks at the foot of the steep
mountainside, sprinkled with miniature pine trees. By habit
I look for *agrimi* here, the wild goats whose ancestors I
have eaten over the years. *Agrimi* are magnificent climbers:
their cloven hooves are specially formed to grip rocks and
they seem to climb for fun. Standing on cliff edges they in-
solently follow my slow progress far below.

Further up the coast I slip inside Nisaki, the little island;
I dive here sometimes and know the layout underwater. I
keep closer to the island than the rocks, but am always
nervous and slow down unnecessarily. I look into the sea
on my port side; a large grouper lives here, too deep for
me to dive and too big for me to shoot. The sea is clear and
I see a shadow, but nothing else. Now comes the wind; the
cliffs are high and once again, it is from the north. Several
hundred metres out it is often calm, a useful thing to know
in a strong wind, but only if you have the courage to pull
away from the coast. I head into the wind fast, so the spray
divides in two and passes my ears. I don't get wet, but
drops land on my glasses and the bright sun confuses my
view. Mavri Petra, Black Rock, where we gather salt and the
stern face of Troulakas slide past. Sometimes I catch barracuda here: once I caught a large tuna and lost a bigger one.
Alona, named for the ancient threshing circles, a confusion
of winds I have learnt to read. The wind comes from the
mountains they say, but it also comes from the cliffs, the
valleys, and even big rocks. There are whooshes and eddies
and spumes of spray and sometimes, if you look carefully,
there is flat sea, offering safety and respite.

Now to Steno, the narrow, dangerous waters that divide
Karpathos from Saria. I keep in to the Karpathos side, shel-
tering behind this rock and that as I chug west, inching
slowly out into the channel. If the engine fails here, or the
propeller is tangled with a plastic bag or fishing line, the
wind and the current will take me hundreds of yards out to

sea in minutes. I touch my anchor as a talisman. I remind myself to lower it carefully if there is a problem and wrap it round a *scarmos*, rowlock, but not too tight or the *scarmos* will break and I could lose hold of the anchor rope and then it is next stop the Lebanon or Israel. But there are no problems and I turn slowly with the wind, *prima* again and head east and inch towards Saria. I slide round its southernmost cape and north again with the wind behind me. Sta Maria, then Asproas, which can be dangerous in a strong wind, and on and up past the rock arch and the cave until finally the sanctuary of Palatia. The journey takes nearly two hours and it is wonderful to arrive alone on an autumn day: to see the old houses and the remans of the fortress high on the left. These ruins are a thousand years old and echo with the sound of insects and the song of *monticola solitarius*, the blue rock thrush. There are domestic goats here and sometimes a shepherd. There could be ghosts. Tourists come here some days and fishermen too, but I prefer to be alone.

One autumn, arriving to work with my bees, I was happy to see Palatia was calm and empty. I anchored and climbed onto the mole with my bags. It was hot, I was tired and took my time lighting the smoker and putting on my boots, jacket, mask and gloves. I climbed slowly up the mountain track, smoked my bees to keep them calm, paused before opening the lid and put food inside. It had been a good summer and there was enough population to keep going through the winter, but it can be cold in Saria and sometimes very wet, so bees need a little nutrition to bridge the time before February or March when the first flowers arrive. As I climbed back down to the valley I saw a fishing boat had arrived, perhaps from Kalymnos. The men were watching me, wondering who this blond guy was with bees and a boat in such a remote place. I packed my things away and got into my boat carefully: determined to show them I knew what I was doing, determined not to make a mistake. I untied, started the engine and began hauling on the anchor rope. This pulled me towards the fishing boat and I realised they had laid their anchor over mine. Watching me carefully they understood their mistake and kindly offered to move their boat:

Tha pame pera?
Ochi tha ftiaxo ego.

That's ok. I will fix it. So I steered my boat under one of their mooring ropes and over another until my anchor was nearly free of theirs. I had to stare into the water to see exactly what I was doing and felt very pleased with myself until. Bump! I hit the fishing boat. Not hard, but etiquette demanded I offered my apologies:

Signomi. Signomi.

And got the reply, in absolutely perfect English, with a Home Counties accent:

That's perfectly all right.

I did not show surprise and neither did he. Off I went, trying to look like a sailor, all the time wandering:

Who was that guy?

I expect he was asking himself the same question.

Antiquas

I find many useful things at sea, some are for my boat, others for the house. In the UK there are complicated laws about the sea and flotsam, which is floating cargo or wreckage, is treated differently from jetsam, which is washed up on the shore. Here there is one rule: on the land it belongs to somebody, at sea it is yours. One time, passing through Steno, I found an aluminium boat hook floating by the coast: a useful prize. I grabbed it and felt pleased with myself as I returned to the village. I anchored my boat under the gaze of a group of children:

That's our granddad's,

they told me. I asked around and identified the grand-dad. It was Iannis. I had a slight acquaintance with the man: he was older than me, proud, with a weather-beaten face; a very strong man. Years ago, after the big flood, we worked together clearing an alleyway of mud and stones. There was only one shovel between us and we took it in turns to fill the wheelbarrow. His turns lasted twice as long and he worked twice as fast as me, so his output was four times mine. Even then I only lasted a morning, whereas he worked all day until the alleyway, some 80 metres long, was clear. I did not know much about him then and did not have the breath to enquire. In any case his accent was very thick and I understood little of what he said, but we became friends. Iannis lives with his wife on the other side of the island, in Tristomo. There is no electricity and water comes from a well, but it is peaceful there and they are happy. They keep sheep and grow fruit and vegetables and when the sea is calm Iannis goes fishing. I respect the man, he is one of the old kind of villager, *chorianos*. I felt guilty at having his boathook and the next time he came to the village I took my prize to him:

Here, Iannis, this is yours.

Where did you find it?

Steno. In the sea.

In the sea?

Yes.

Then it's yours.

And no matter how hard I tried he would not accept his boathook back. He will accept a drink now and again and he does tell me stories. One dates from before the war, from the time of the Italians, or even from the time of the Turks. Ancient artefacts and antiques were rapidly growing in value in those days and traders were going round the islands scooping up what they could. One, a wily dealer, came in a *caique* from Rhodos. There was no harbour in Diafani in those days and no road up to Olymbos, but he was well prepared and sent leaflets ahead of him to *to chorio*. These told that at a certain time he would be at the *megaron* and would buy *antiquas*, old things. He had heard there was old, valuable furniture in the village so hired donkeys to fetch it back. The entourage of merchant, servants and donkeys went up the old path to the village in the mountains; it is a steep climb and they took two hours in the heat of the day, but eventually they arrived in the village and made their way to the hall. In the days before television this was a big event and quite a crowd was waiting: no women, no young people, just men: old men. The merchant arranged for cool, fresh water to be brought, glasses and coffee and *ouzo*. He then went into a big speech, explaining he was an honest man and would give good money for *antiquas*. Who would be the first to come forward? Who would be the first to get a handful of money? Nobody moved, so he ordered a servant to pour more *ouzo*. This was fun: the old men laughed and smiled and drank their drinks and looked on expectantly. The dealer became impassioned, explained that he loved beautiful objects and it was a shame to keep them in dank, dark houses when they could be in shops and museums. And the money was good. But nobody came forward. More *ouzo*, this time with *meze*, more sales pitch and still no *antiquas*. The dealer was suspicious and getting angry. He had spent several days and lots of *drachmes* to come to this god-forsaken place and he knew there were antiques hidden in the village. Eventually he raised his voice:

> Where are the *antiquas*? I know you have them. Where are the *antiquas*?

The old men looked at one another. This was a stranger, they had accepted his hospitality, they had to explain. One of the oldest men leant forward. The dealer strained to understand what he was saying:

> *Antiquas*? We are *antiquas*. We are the most *antiqua* in the village.

And they laughed and laughed and laughed as did Iannis many decades later as he told me the story. His eyes gleamed and his teeth flashed as he poured another *ouzo*:

> We are all *antiquas* now.

Killing Eagles

Rural people in Greece have different sensibilities to the northern visitors who come and stay in the summer. There are few pets in the village because animals, like humans, must earn their keep. Some men keep dogs to hunt hare and partridges, but they don't last long on the harsh, abrasive mountainsides. In the old days when dogs were thought too old, they would be taken out to sea and thrown overboard. If they made it back to land then a mistake had been made and the old dog would be reprieved for another season. These days they are more likely to be shot. As *to chorio* gets richer and is influenced by the outside world, sensibilities change, but very few villagers share my respect and love for wild creatures: they think of me as eccentric, or mad, or both.

Some years back, after an extended and severe storm, a Dalmatian pelican was stranded in the village. The villagers asked me if it could be eaten. I explained it would not make good soup and said it was a special bird suffering from lack of food due to the weather. Only then did the fishermen open their freezers and feed frozen fish to a confused and hungry animal. It remained in the village all summer before moving south to Pigadia where it stayed another two years before wandering off again.

The Bonelli's, *aquila fasciata*, is a medium sized eagle with a wingspan of around 165 centimetres. Endangered, with fewer than 1000 pairs worldwide, there are less than 100 pairs in Greece. We have at least one pair on the north of the island and I have taken it upon myself to keep an eye on them. They are creatures of habit and, depending on the weather, I can normally find them. Everyone knows, or wants to know, your business in the village and the shepherds and farmers know my interests and tell me when they have seen these birds. A few years ago a pair took to roosting in the church tower. Every time the bell rang, pigeons would fly out. Every time the pigeons appeared, so would a Bonnelli and bang, a flutter of feathers and lunch is served in the belfry. Few tourists noticed this phenomenon, but the local children made videos on their mobile phones. After a few months either the eagles got bored with celebrity, or the pigeon population declined and the Bonelli's moved elsewhere. In the past the local shepherds saw Bonelli's as rivals: eagles would take the occasional lamb so they had to be scared away, or killed. My friend Iannis killed one with his bare hands when he was young. The Bonnelli had been taking his lambs and food was scarce: people on the island were starving. Iannis knew where the nest was; he climbed the cliff and ran towards the bird sitting on eggs. The bird did not flee, but attacked Iannis sinking its talons into his arm. There was a lot of blood, but the battle was one sided: even a bird as large as a Bonelli only weighs a few kilos, Iannis was and is, fearless and he killed the bird with his bare hands. Europeans will recoil at this act, but they were different and difficult times and moralities change:

I wouldn't do it these days.

Iannis told me, and it is true; the local people have begun to appreciate the power and grace of these magnificent birds.

The fishermen who come to the village have a difficult life and work hard, but they have little knowledge of fish, no affection for marine mammals and view Monk seals and dolphins as direct threats to their livelihood and life. If they see a seal or dolphin near their boats their first instinct is to shoot them with their high powered rifles. Monk seals are extremely rare animals, there are perhaps forty in the area, though this estimate is tentative. They range hundreds of miles looking for food or fun, or both and return to select caves to give birth to their young. These seals are inquisitive and friendly animals and this has led to their demise. We often see them in the harbour where they come to fish and maybe pick up the news from the *cafeneion*. They rest in caves along the coast, watching the movement of boats till they lazily wobble into the sea leaving behind them the pungent stench of seal piss and fishy farts.

Playful animals with mournful eyes, Monk seals sometimes dive and surface either side of my boat when I am anchored in the harbour. I have to chase them away or they become too trusting of man. As dolphins do, they make big holes in fishing nets when scavenging trapped fish and this is one reason they are shot. Another is that being fish eaters they are rivals to fishermen who exaggerate their impact on the fish stock, feel there are less fish in the sea to catch and sell and less of a chance to afford a flat-screen television. There is a program, based in the village, to protect Monk seals and I spend a lot of time talking to fishermen to persuade them not to molest these animals. Some have been persuaded, but others are sceptical and believe we have a boat full of baby seals and one day we will come over the horizon and start throwing them into the sea. If only.

A Young Girl in the Village

Tourists are attracted to the village by dreams. One dream is nurtured by the everyday clothes of the older women: supposedly timeless, traditional symbols of a bygone age, in the argot of the tourist brochure. Their dress consists of a black *kavai* and apron worn over long white cotton underpants and shifts. These are often coupled with *stivania,* the long leather boots so useful on thorny mountainsides. In the hot weather, while working in the fields, or early in the morning around the narrow lanes where I live, the women discard the *kavai* and walk around in their voluminous underclothes.

Boots are expensive items and hot so the women take them off when ploughing. Tourists know nothing of these foibles and nothing about the women. I don't think they care about reality, just the dream. I too am ignorant, but over the years I have learned to treat the older women with respect: they are hardworking, funny, raucous and ribald, but also cunning and suspicious; they should never, ever be underestimated and it pays to take care when discussing fellow villagers as they may be related. One loose word about a first or second cousin, a nephew, husband or brother-in-law can lead to serious grief.

In order to renew their ties and introduce their children into the communal network many villagers return in the summer from their place of exile. This is the time for marriages and baptisms and tourists are sometimes lucky to see young girls dressed in colourful *kavai* or *sakofoustano,* the brightly coloured blouse and skirt embroidered with sewn ribbons and gaudy colours. Sometimes the girls wear *pantofles*, locally produced leather slippers that slip and click as they dance and provide a measure of syncopation to the music. On such occasions the eldest unmarried daughter will wear a single gold coin on a chain round her neck or even a row of necklaces, *kolaina*, made up of sovereigns, doubloons and other heavy gold coins. Amid the colourful crowd the observant will sometimes hear girls who may speak a little Greek, but prefer English which they deliver with a Brooklyn or Canadian accent. There are even girls with perfect American manners and voices and no Greek at all. Others are dialect speakers from *to chorio* or Saria. Talk to them and you will find they are thoughtful, impressive young people, but nobody has bothered to tell their story. One local girl told me in pure Baltimore dialect:

> You have totally gotten into the habits and the mentality of Karpathians. Things which to us are quite obvious, but for an outsider must seem so awkward. You should write something about how the girls of the village feel.

I am old and a man and cannot possibly do that, but I can allow them to speak for themselves. I have disguised their voices as they have been open with me and I don't want to cause problems with their family: especially their formidable mothers. Here, gently edited, are the voices of the girls of *to chorio*:

> I was born in America and specifically in Baltimore, Maryland... As you know there are a lot of Olimbites in Baltimore, most of them own pizza parlours and restaurants or sub shops (cheese steaks). They are all decent people and earned each and every penny they have. My father owned a small restaurant with his two brothers. Most of their life was work-work-work.

My dad had a passion for food, he loves cooking so he worked 17 hours a day.

Life at home was very traditional, we went to a private school to get the best education and in the afternoons all of the Greek children and Karpathakia went to Greek school. We were taught Greek dances, Greek history, and grammar. My life was more relaxing and fun than it would have been in London or Rhodes. We used to meet up somewhere, sometimes in my aunt's house where we would dance to Greek music and sing and play games while our parents sat in the kitchen talking.

People from Olymbos were all a big family; there was trust and love and no envy whatsoever. This compares well with village life here which is dominated by envy and competition. We used to go to the Karpathian *syllogos,* association, every Saturday where we learned how to dance and sing village songs.

My uncle was one of the *archi-meraklides,* senior musicians, of the village. He taught my brother and I to dance *sousta, zervo,* and *pano choro* and he wrote down the lyrics of the old songs so we could sing them the right way. In the village the songs alter over the years. When we came back from America we corrected what they sing here. The old people tell us we get it right. We had an old black cassette player and we played it and laughed and danced every day. We still continued all the traditions: we wore our outfits on special occasions and the Greek spirit was so high.

We went to church every Sunday; everything a true Karpathian would do except in a twentieth century country. All the ladies there continued cross-stitching

and sewing as a hobby; they bought fancy materials
and made us the traditional outfit. My mother baked
bread as often as she could, and of course only
cooked Greek food. That's how we spent our days.
Everyone's goal was to move back to Greece. Even
when I was 6-7 years old I remember aiming for good
marks at school so I could get 10 dollars from my dad
to put in the piggy bank to go towards a ticket to Karpathos.

If my parent's could not come with us to the village,
they would send us every summer and we would stay
for at least three months here with my *giagiades*,
grandmothers and *papoudes*, grandfathers. Awhhh, it
was a dream come true whenever we would get in
the boat from Rhodes to Karpathos. My *giagia* was so
happy each time....she force fed us until we felt
sick...she went to the truck that brings the fruit every
week and bought everything he had, from peanuts to
spinach. She even brought us 2 boxes of coca-cola,
each time she went shopping, as a way of saying that
she wanted us to feel at home. I remember the summers; there were a lot of children here, much more
than now and we spent our days on the beach playing and diving from the mole. I remember my *giagia*
shouting at us to get out of the sea and come home.
The older children would light fires on the beach and
we would sit with our cassette player and sing and
cook octopus *souvlaki* and eat things we had taken
from home.

I still remember those days. We were happy and
carefree. When we moved back to Greece everything
changed; suddenly I didn't feel as "Greek" as I used to
feel when I was in America. I didn't go to church and
there was no sing-song in the parlour. Of course I

was older, but it wasn't the same, though my mom kept taking us to the *syllogos* as usual. All my Saturdays from my childhood were in a *syllogos* dancing and singing our music. We lived in Athens but came back to the village every Christmas, Easter and summer.

Another girl:

I was born in Canada. My parents went there so that I and my brothers would have Canadian passports and have a good future. About love and arranged marriages? Things are quite obvious. If we marry outside the village we will upset our parents. Boys can do as they like, as they are considered superior, they can go out with women and they are encouraged to do so. On the other hand women are told that if a guy looks at us we should turn our back and don't even speak to him, because the only thing they want from us is sex.

My aunt says that a man on the first date will take you out for a coffee, on the second for lunch, on a third to the cinema and the next date is sex... heheh, so we should avoid all men, they are bad and they can harm us! From what I can tell, my mom has someone in mind for me in the future and also for my brothers. It is common sense for mothers to think about who would most be suitable for their daughters, but they never talk about who they like or which family likes us. Its all a mystery. I will be told when there is a successful candidate and then I will get my say. There are, shall we say, criteria: they look at the family...if he comes from a great *genia* ...if he has a nice job. Only LAWYERS and DOCTORS are considered a a nice job. If he is *gennishmos* which means if his family has a history of being barren or reproductively challenged..heheh. If his family are *meraklides*, if they like going to Karpathos and the *glendia*, festivities. If he has *proika*, dowry, if he has a house or two I suppose would be ok and of course if he is handsome because they won't want the family name to be carried down by ugly children.

Another:

My view is that you can have a successful family even if you marry someone you don't love. A nice marriage between a man and a woman is having the same values, understanding and respect for each other and then love will grow. I am not saying that when you fall in love with someone and you have a family it will not be successful, only that love fades away, the passion goes and then you are left with the respect for each other and everything you have done together. I might be influenced in this by my parents and their views on marriage as they want me to marry a Karpathian.

Although of course I am not allowed to speak to anyone apart from cousins, so how am I going to meet him? I avoid everyone who is a male Karpathian, I only have male friends who are not Karpathians. I know one day I may be brainwashed into marrying a guy I don't even know and have never heard of and the idea freaks me out. On the other hand I wouldn't want to let down my parent's and marry someone who is not from here because it is like a disgrace to the family. My parent's got married with an arranged marriage and it has worked out brilliantly. I hope I have a marriage like that. I have seen a lot of women of my mom's age whose marriages have worked out perfectly. 90-95% are successful, but then again, men and women were different those days...they were un-educate: they didn't know better, they hadn't been outside Karpathos until they got married. Nowadays many women in the village have at least a Bachelor's and some of them a Masters and they are powerful and successful in what they do. Things have changed and I don't think arranged marriages will exist in 50 years.

Another:

The way a marriage is arranged, I am not an ex-pert.....if a family is interested in marrying a son to a girl, the family goes to her house and they talk it through. I know that at 15th of August, on the day of the big festival, all the old ladies look at the girls that are free and they match them with who they think would be interested. Its like dating on the internet. Then they talk it through with the guy, they take him a picture of the girl and if he wants to get married with her, they take his photograph to the girl and so on.

Women as they grow older are all about their family and relatives... They cook and clean the house, all day they look after their husband and children... they always put money at the side for a difficulty that might arise.... they are *noikokures*, housewives. When they see their children doing well it is confirmation that they have raised them properly. What pleases them most is when someone comes from the *cafeneion* and says:

I saw your son today and what a smart gentleman he is.

And when the son or daughter have jobs they are good oikogeneiarxes, they protect their family. Parents show their love not with presents, but with the way they protect you and the way they talk to you. When a son or a daughter gives them a grandson or granddaughter they go crazy, they are so proud they glow. When my parent's brought my brother Manolis to the village my grandfather would ask everyone for fresh eggs and fresh katsikisio gala, goats milk, to feed him. He would run around to chorio to find the best of everything and go to to molo for the best fish. He used to lift Manolis on his shoulders and walk around with him, hand in hand. Manolis was a cute baby, treated as a celebrity in the village and Anna at the cafeneion would give him sweets. There is a saying in Greece "tou paidiou mou to paidi dyo fores paidi" meaning "my child's child is twice my child."

Another:

In the old days the eldest daughter would inherit everything from her mother and as there was a bride price agreed before marriage the money would end up with the women. Maybe that's why the older generation of women is so strong. Nowadays the *proika* is up to the parents... my mom for example will divide everything equally among the children. Other parents are different, for example my aunt has 3 daughters and a son and she gave most of her estate to the first daughter who also got money and some fields from her grand mom. The second daughter got some olive trees and the third was given a flat in Rhodes. The boy, she says, can work hard and make his own money. But his uncle never had children and gave him some of the things he owned before he was married. It depends on the parents mainly. If they are fair or not. I know a lady who had two daughters and four sons. Only one son and the two daughters got something: the other boys were given some old olive trees. Life here is difficult for an only child. There is so much pressure on a girl. She has to do the right thing. I will be married soon and I am so excited. I have wanted him ever since I was very young and when I heard he was interested I just couldn't believe it. I could not believe it was true.

Finally, and perhaps sadly:

Those of us brought up in America or Athens or Rhodes, go out for coffee and to clubs and have fun with our friends. Then we come to the village and we feel restricted; we pretty much have to stay in the house watching TV, especially when it is Christmas or Easter. Even in summer we have to watch how we speak and look and react. We put on the mask of a serious *Karpathia*, someone who has no life of her own. I wish things were different for us. Personally I adore Diafani and Olympos with all the hidden beauties, but it seems as if I can't be free here. I feel as if I'm in Big Brother and a camera is looking at everything I do.

Humour

I suppose the characteristic I most love about the village is the humour. Each day brings a stream of quips, jokes, asides and one-liners. Even at the height of a row, someone will say something that cracks me up. Outsiders are often the butt of jokes, but the villagers also laugh at themselves. In an attempt to minimise corruption the government has decreed that coast guards and the regular police are not stationed in their home region. Sometimes this creates social tension as the incomers are in a position of power, but have little feeling for local customs and traditions. One time, the head of the port police was having a massive row with Dinos, at that time the deputy mayor. A crowd gathered round as he shouted at Dinos:

All you people want is anarchy.

To which Dinos replied:

Ah, now you are beginning to understand us.

The crowd laughed and the argument stopped.

Another time, Dino's brother had been celebrating at a wedding. Very much the worse for wear he spied me as my section of the crowd dragged me past his entourage. We had not met for over a year and he greeted me with:

Giassou Jinks. Give me a kiss!

Well, it is Greece, so I gave him a kiss. On the cheeks. With a broad grin he challenged my English reserve, demanding:

On the lips!

So, I kissed him on the lips. But he upped the ante, demanding:

Give me your tongue!

And we collapsed in giggles and do so every time we meet.

Some of the jokes go on for a long time. A cuddly, grey haired bachelor, had two left feet as a young man, but still fancied himself as a footballer. Thirty years later he is known universally as...Pele.

Others are spontaneous. One afternoon I was walking down from the village. The community bus had broken down, was parked by the road and a pair of feet were poking out from underneath. It was Michaelis from Olymbos:

Are you ok Michaelis?

Yes, I always spend my afternoons under a bus.

The women here are a separate race with their own mores, culture and language. They have a fine sense of humour and constantly indulge in word play. This takes time to translate, but it is worth a try. There is a kind man in the village, a painter and decorator, an Egyptian. Given the state of the world and their lack of wit the men started to call him Bin Laden. The women rarely use consonants, so Bin Laden became Billae and soon morphed into Billy. And last I heard they had added the translation into Greek, so now he is called Vassilly. A fine name for an Egyptian.

A story from long ago involves the school bell. Greek education has never been noted for its sophistication and until recent times it was thought that children deliberately failed to learn and the only antidote to ignorance was a good beating, or some other punishment. Look around the village any time of day or night. Normally it is calm and quiet: old men sit in chairs outside the *cafeneion* while women sit in the shade, watching and waiting for something to happen. I will not tell you his name, but one man will be on the move, always on the move: bar to bar, restaurant to restaurant, this group of tourists to that group over there; a perpetual motion machine he is active all day long.

Now a hardworking, upright citizen and hotel owner he was in his younger days a terrible scholar: he did not like school and he did not like the schoolteacher and saw no use for book learning. Consequentially he stayed in bed as long as he could and was always late for class in the morning. In those days there were few clocks in the village and the schoolteacher would ring the school bell fifteen minutes before class began to summon his pupils. The teacher was a cruel man and chose a cruel punishment for the tardy boy: from now on the boy would get up early and he would ring the bell. Or be beaten. The teacher would stay in bed an extra fifteen minutes.

It must not be assumed that being bad at school has much to do with intelligence. The lazy boy was very smart and he was determined to triumph over authority. He thought and puzzled to find a way out of his predicament; the school was hundreds of metres from his house and it took three days for the solution to present itself; three days of getting up early to ring the bell for his fellow pupils. My friend comes from a seafaring family and had access to lines and cords and weights and pulleys. He checked out angles and corners, relative heights, quiet paths and empty lots. He waited till dark before going about his mysterious business. Come dawn he was in bed, awaiting the hour. The bedroom window was open and a thin cord stretched out and along and up and over roofs and walls until it reached the clapper of the school bell. He tugged gently, then again with more vigour until he heard that wonderful sound.

Ding-dong, ding-dong, ding-dong, and another fifteen minutes in bed.

Some jokes are taken to extreme lengths. I was walking to the harbour to meet my son, Sion, off the ferry boat: it was early spring and he was coming over for an out of season holiday. Somehow I picked up with Iannis Minatsis at the edge of the village and we walked together. Coincidentally he was supposed to meet his son, but on the way his mobile rang and it was his son explaining there was a change of plan and he was coming three days later. So we went to meet Sion together. We were the only people on the harbour. The ferry boat arrived, spun round without the aid of ropes or anchor, lowered the *pantofla*, slipper, or ramp and off strode Sion. I introduced him to Iannis, who offered to carry his bag and as we walked back to the village Iannis explained that his son was coming from Canada in the next few days, they were the same age and he was sure they would make a *parea,* company. He also revealed this was a son from his first marriage and it would be his first visit to the village. Iannis' current wife had never met her stepson and she would be organising a party. We arrived at the Rahati and sat down for a drink. I left for home after one beer. Sion didn't arrive so, after a couple of hours I went back to the Rahati to find him. He wasn't there and neither was Iannis:

Where's Iannis?

Gone up to Olympos with his son.

His son didn't come.

Yes he did. They came here for a drink. Iannis' wife rang. They have gone up the hill for the party.

But...

What could I say? Someone had seen Iannis carrying my son's bag, had assumed my son was his son, phoned the wife, to explain your stepson is here and.....

Two days later, Sion appeared at my house. He had a headache. He told me that it was a hell of a party and while they had not killed a fatted calf, they had roasted a goat, as befits a prodigal son in Greece. For some reason Sion has changed his name to Elias. We are still on good terms.

Finally an old joke, probably a 1000 years or more. I was talking to Antonis in the Gorgona restaurant and telling him my life would be much improved if I had a small table I could use as a desk. He asked me what size I wanted and I explained it had to be this, by that, by that, made of wood and, to cap off the request, it had to be blue. Antonis thought for a while, then asked me to step outside. He pointed to the back of a truck and asked what I could see inside. There it was: a blue, wooden table, this by that, by that. Antonis is a generous man and told me the table was mine for free, so long as I did not take it until I had eaten. He wandered off into the dark and I went back to my meal. Half an hour later I hoisted the table above my head and zig-zagged home. On the way I passed Antonis in the *cafeneion*. I waved, but he ignored me. The following night I sought out my benefactor to buy him a drink:

What's this for?

And I told him it was for the table. He started to laugh and explained that because of me he was 100 euros better off. He had won a bet:

Sitting in Anna's last night I bet that in the next ten minutes we would see an Englishmen carrying a blue, wooden table.

From that day I do not take bets in the village.

World War Two

Major events like wars and revolutions resonate in different ways, create their own myths and carry different messages. The conflict between the Allies and the Axis powers is known as World War Two in Britain and some say it started on September 1 1939 with the German invasion of Poland. Others have the start date as September 3rd, when Britain and France declared war on Germany. Often forgotten is that Russia, with the agreement of Hitler, attacked Poland 16 days later. The war between Russia and Nazi Germany and its allies is called the Great Patriotic War by the Russians and their dates are from June 22 1941 to May 9 1945. Italy declared war on France and Britain on June 10 1940 and after a disastrous war, signed a secret armistice with the Allies on September 3 1943, whereupon, a few days later, hostilities broke out between Germany and parts of the Italian state.

Continuing the story for other combatant nations: on December 7 1941 Japan attacked the British in Malaya and the United States' naval base at Pearl Harbor and four days later Hitler declared war on the United States. The period could be better described as the Second World Wars and it is important to keep some of the dates in mind. Recently in Britain two prime ministers have tried to rewrite history for their own purposes. Tony Blair explained that Britain should stand by America as they stood by Britain in the Blitz, the sustained bombing of Britain by Nazi Germany, which had finished months before America, reluctantly, entered the war. More recently David Cameron claimed that Britain was the junior partner to the US in the war against Germany in 1940, 'though the US was not in the war at that time.

On the night of 27 October 1940 Emanuele Grazzi, the Italian ambassador to Greece, went to a party at the German embassy in Athens. Perhaps, it was something he drank, or maybe he was following instruction from Mussolini, but at dawn the following day he presented an ultimatum to Metaxas, the dictator of Greece, demanding access to strategic areas of the country. Supposedly Metaxas replied *Alors, c'est la guerre*, then it is war, but the popular view is that he replied with the single Greek word *Ochi* meaning No! and every year in Greece, October 28 is celebrated as *Ochi* day. At 5.30 am Italy invaded Greece from the then Italian protectorate of Albania and the Greek-Italian war began. The first that the population of Greece heard about the outbreak of hostilities was the despatch from the General staff read out on Athens Radio:

> Since 05:30 this morning, the enemy is attacking our vanguard on the Greek-Albanian border. Our forces are defending the fatherland.

Shortly afterwards, Metaxas addressed the Greek people:

> The time has come for Greece to fight for her independence. Greeks, now we must prove ourselves worthy of our forefathers and the freedom they bestowed upon us. Now, above all, the struggle!

Greeks never miss an opportunity to quote from the ancients and the last sentence is verbatim from *The Persians* by Aeshylus, a play first performed in 470 BC! Greece was a divided country in 1940, the Communist party was outlawed and its leaders imprisoned, but Greeks are patriots and the population went out to the streets singing patriotic

songs and shouting anti-Italian slogans. Hundreds of thousands of volunteers, both men and women, queued to
enlist at Greek Army offices and for a time the whole nation
was united in the face of aggression. The Italian invasion
plan was a farce. Under Mussolini's orders Generals Pietro
Badoglio and Mario Roatta had recently demobilised
600,000 men to help gather the harvest in Italy! Now, they
were given twelve days notice of an invasion.

The front was 150 km long, divided by the Pindus
mountains, with few roads, none of them suitable for
mechanised warfare; winter set in early and conditions
were atrocious. With men and women fighting at altitude in
snow and ice the Greek resistance was truly heroic. The
Italians were defeated, giving the Allies their first land victory of the war. In April 1941 Hitler was forced to send
German forces to overcome Greece, thus delaying the
planned invasion of the Soviet Union by a crucial, perhaps
fatal, six weeks. The delay allowed General Winter, to para-
phrase Tsar Nickolas I, to play its part and the German advance into Russia to be halted. Given this was an industrial
war it is ironic to note that one reason for the delay was
that Hitler did not have enough horses and mules to service his armies in Greece and Russia at the same time.

Little of this drama is appreciated or understood in
depth by the people of *to chorio*. Seventy years ago there
was sparse communication between the village and the
outside world: there was no road between Olymbos and
Diafani nor to the south of the island; transport was by
mule and donkey, telephones were rare and not one electric light shone at night time. No matter what the Treaty of
Lausanne said, the villagers knew they were Greeks and
when the Greek government said *Ochi* to the Italian de-
mand they had to respond.

Armed resistance on the island was out of the question.
It is possible to resist and fight in the landscape of the

north, but impossible to live there without massive support from the villages and that would put the inhabitants at risk. Technically the people were Italian citizens and resistance was an act of treason. The people agreed to oppose the Italian occupation passively; which they did with great success. The women took the lead: lying, cheating and confusing the Italians as if they had been doing it all their lives; one time they even took up arms in the form of the long and heavy tools they use while baking at their wood burning ovens.

For the young men it was difficult. Many of them felt they had to join the struggle and slowly, in ones and twos and threes, they sneaked away from the island and made their way to the mainland to enrol in the army or join the *andartes* in the mountains. Heroic voyages were made in impossibly small boats across the Aegean: one four metre boat powered by oars and sail journeyed from Piraeus to Turkey and its crew of four eventually ended up in Egypt where they enlisted in the Greek army. 63 young men from *to chorio* joined the fight. Some came back years or decades later, others did not return at all. There is a monument to these men at the entrance to the village.

One weapon of passive resistance, as always, was ridicule. There is a wonderful *mantinada* commonly known as *Signiori Brigandiere* composed by Georgos Manios a leading *meraklis* and father of our old friend Kosmas. If you ask, Kosmas will sing it for you. Some time in late 1940 the villagers were summoned to perform at a festival to celebrate the arrival of the new Italian military commander. They could not decline the invitation and were unsure what to do, even up to the point when Georgos started to sing. The first line of the *mantinada* sounded harmless enough, but on closer listening to the dialect it contained several levels of meaning. The simplest translation starts:

A thousand welcomes *Signorei Brigandiere*, may you
never see your homeland again.

And continues in the same ironic tone. Of course, when
he started to sing, none of the villagers knew what to expect and when the words came out they were greeted with
cheers and laughter and they all joined in the chorus:

Never see your homeland again.
Never see your homeland again.

The Italian commander was very pleased to see these
simple people giving him such a genuine welcome.

Karpathos was not entirely peaceful: there was privation
and oppression, even murders and atrocities. Some mothers dressed their sons as girls as they were frightened the
Germans would take male children away. Others breast fed
their malnourished children until they were eight or nine
years old. These were peasant people, they survived any
way they could.

Grain and flour were confiscated to feed the occupiers
and pack animals requisitioned, forcing human beings to
do the carrying work of animals. One story tells of a mur-
dered man being buried and later dug up so his
neighbours could retrieve his boots, others tell of collabo-
ration between the richer elements of the population and
the Italian occupiers.

As the war raged across North Africa, Karpathos assumed
an important strategic location; in 1942 the Germans in-
stalled a primitive radar and listening post on a mountain
above Pigadia, while the Italians had an observation post
and anti aircraft position on the peak between Diafani and
Avlona. In early September 1943, while the Allies and the
Italians were negotiating an armistice, the Germans began
to exert pressure on Italian forces in the Dodecanese.

German seaplanes landed on the lagoon at Tristomo, they were fired on by the Italian garrison and the crews captured and taken to Pigadia.

Days later German troops landed from Crete and forcefully, though without bloodshed, seized control of the island from the Italians. Captain Bethege, the German battalion commander, became the military governor: he left the Italians in charge of the police and civil administration, but they had very little power. For personal reasons around 100 of the Italian forces elected to serve under the German command: they had wives and girlfriends, even children on the island and wanted to stay. The remaining Italian military personnel, approximately 4000, were placed in a concentration camp with the promise of repatriation to Italy. A few hundred at a time were shipped to Crete and from there to the Greek mainland 'though many Italians were not allowed home, but sent to forced labour camps in Germany. During the sea crossings, several hundred prisoners lost their lives to Allied aircraft and submarines. Several prisoners escaped from the concentration camp and, with the help of local people, hid in the mountains, but the life was too hard, the locals could not support them and most eventually gave up and surrendered to the Germans. One soldier was captured and executed. Another, with the help of a local family, survived outside the village. For many years after the war he returned for his summer holidays, each time, to the delight of the locals, bringing a different girlfriend.

In the confusion of the Italian surrender many Karpathians stole weapons: they were hidden away, but hardly used in anger. Gradually the skies became controlled by the Allies and most of the seas. Various allied special forces arrived to watch and observe the German troop movements. One attachment was located north of the village at Vananda and were fed and entertained by local people. In return they gave hope for the future and cigarettes. The latter proved to be dangerous gifts. There is a story that one careless villager was smoking in the *cafeneion*, the commander of the German forces stationed in the village recognised a foreign smell and the man was beaten savagely.

As the fighting intensified in the autumn of 1943 there were several air and sea engagements around the island. Aircraft on both sides were shot down and cargo and warships sunk, some of them close to the shore. There was little respite for the inhabitants of Karpathos: many of the young men were away, leaving women, children and old people to gather in the harvest. They were forced to feed the German army for little compensation and consequently food was scarce. Under Italian rule it had been decreed that teaching had to be in Italian and Greek schools were closed. To relieve friction with the indigenous population the Germans reversed this ruling and in January 1944 Greek teachers were hired and schools reopened, though materials were scarce and teachers went unpaid.

However, the tide of war was changing and Allied naval and air forces based in Egypt and Cyprus were increasing their grip on the sea and sky. Pigadia came under regular attack, seaplanes and small craft were sunk in the harbour and larger craft further out to sea. Small islands to the west of Rhodes were occupied by Allied forces from time to time and although these incursions were unsuccessful there was much talk of an imminent invasion of Karpathos. A patrol from the Greek Holy Squadron even landed on the west coast of the Karpathos, but sustained casualties and was forced to withdraw.

The German army was spread thinly over most of Europe and on August 31 1944 Hitler decided to concentrate on the defence of Germany. The evacuation from Karpathos started a few days later, first to Rhodes and then to the Greek mainland. Harassed all the way, their boats were attacked and some never made it as far as Rhodes. Once again Karpathos was left in the hands of the Italian police and civil administration, but only for a brief period. The local population formed a Revolutionary Committee and after negotiation with the Italians, took control of the island.

This was a period of maximum danger for the people of the island: during the years of foreign occupation it was necessary to co-operate, to some extent, with the alien forces who, after all, were the ones with the power and the guns. Undoubtedly some took this co-operation too far and took advantage of the situation for personal advancement. Now blood could be spilt and old scores could be settled, but Karpathians are surprisingly gentle people and the island avoided the civil conflict that occurred elsewhere in Greece.

One of the first acts of the Revolutionary Committee was to declare unification with Greece, an understandable act, but one which led to complications and conflict with the Allies. On October 9 a six and a half metre sailing boat set off from Finiki with seven men to sail to Egypt to inform the Allies the Germans had left and the island was liberated. It took them five days in stormy seas, but the message got through.

The men returned on October 17 with the Royal Navy. The British destroyers Terpsichore and Cleveland sailed into Pigadia and with 27 commandos took over the administration of the island in the name of the Allies. There was some chaos with road blocks scattered around and bands of armed men searching the countryside looking for non-existent spies. On October 28 the cruiser Black Prince arrived with 300 Indian soldiers of the splendidly named Maharaja of Gwalior battalion commanded by Major Singh.

However it was Captain Pyke who was in overall command of Karpathos. He had with him several British officers who took control of the legal, civic and commercial life of the island. The Karpathians wanted Greek law to apply immediately, but acting under instructions, Captain Pyke would not allow this and the law of the occupying forces prevailed. Malnutrition was rife and the distribution of flour and other foodstuffs was urgently required. Rhodes remained under German control for eight months after the liberation of Karpathos, but the Germans could not provide for the islanders and there was widespread malnutrition and even starvation. As many as 4000 refugees arrived on Karpathos to be fed and sheltered by the British administration. Following the surrender of the Germans the refugees returned to Rhodes in April and May 1945. In the summer of 1946, the British organised local elections on Karpathos, whilst the future of the Dodecanese was being decided at the post war peace conference in Paris.

On February 10 1947 a Peace Treaty between Greece and Italy was signed, which finally turned the Dodecanese over to Greece. On March 31 1947 Admiral Pericles Ioannidis was appointed the military governor of the Dodecanese and lieutenant Panagiotis Psomopoulos took over the military administration of Karpathos. It had taken 600 years, but Karpathos was finally united with Greece.

John Pyke

Winston Churchill is considered a great war leader and a fine strategist. Apart from the strange aberration that led him to oppose the Normandy landings of June 6th 1944, this verdict is broadly correct. But, he had been an officer in the cavalry, he romanticised the cut and thrust of small scale skirmishes and to the despair of the strategists who worked closely with him, loved to meddle, sometimes with disastrous results. In 1943 his attention focused on the Eastern Mediterranean. Churchill was obsessed with the idea that if the Italians could be persuaded to join with the British and throw the Germans out of the Dodecanese, the Turks would side with the allies and British bombers could use bases in Turkey to attack the Romanian airfields currently fuelling Hitler's war effort.

Under instruction from Churchill, but against the wishes of the Army, the Navy and the Royal Air Force, the British planned a half hearted and half-cocked invasion of Rhodes and attempted the occupation of Kos, Leros and Samos. This led to the humiliating defeat of British and Allied forces at the hands of better led, better trained and better equipped Germans. Even if the venture had resulted in a clear victory of the Allies in the Dodecanese it would have made no difference to the progress of the war as bombers were not guarantors of victory. In any case, the German position was strengthened, many Italians were massacred and all the British forces were shown to be inadequate.

Churchill's interest was excited by the numerous exotic and peripheral units operating in the area since 1940. Often led by eccentric grandees and public-school boys, they captured Churchill's belligerent imagination in private meetings in the Cabinet War Rooms in London's Whitehall. The units included the Special Air Service, the Special Boat Section, the Long Range Desert Group and Popski's Private Army as well as the SOE and other fringe operators of the Army, Navy and Air Force. Sometimes foolhardy, often ineffectual, but certainly brave, elements of these units roamed the area by *caique*, were transported by submarine or dropped by parachute.

I have known two of these brave men and the story of one of them follows below. Captain John Pyke could have been given his name by Shakespeare. It described him perfectly. I was introduced to him by Anthony Papalas who has a relationship with the island of Ikaria as I have with Karpathos. He knew that John had been in Karpathos during the war and arranged for me to visit him. What follows is my recollection of the meeting and John's recollection of part of his war. Those who wish to delve further will find that his wartime ventures have been well documented: see Rebels and Radicals by Papalas and the Aegean Adventures of Captain John Pyke by Mike Beckett. John Pyke died a few months after we met. He was a lovely man.

John Pyke looks good for his 94 years. His body is wasted by old age, but he stands straight and looks me in the eye as he takes my hand and welcomes me into the sitting room. Since his wife died John Pyke lives alone: everything in its place, everything tidied away, all surfaces dusted, much as you would expect from an army man. When I telephoned he told me to come early afternoon so we could have a cup of tea, or maybe something a little stronger. We settle for Coca Cola.

The window of the sitting room looks out over the waters to the hills and mountains of North Wales. The view is beautiful and poignant. I have a home in those hills:

So, I hear you were in Karpathos during the war.

That's right, I went all over the Dodecanese.

Were you in Diafani?

No, somebody else was there. I was in the South. At the port. What's its name?

Pigadia

I tell him, perhaps a little too quickly:

That's right.

When were you there?

1943.

There is a pause. There must be a mistake. He is old, maybe he is confused:

Are you sure? The Italians were still there in 1943.

That's right. That's right. But they didn't bother me.

The Italians were more or less, out of the war at the time of his arrival, though some elements were siding with the Germans, but the Dodecanese were technically and legally Italian and the Italians still occupied Karpathos. John Pyke was a member of the Special Boat Service, a commando. His brief was to roam the Aegean and keep an eye on the Germans. He was given a small *caique* with a Greek crew and set off from Alexandria. I think he arrived in uniform.

What did you do when you arrived in Pigadia?

Well, I found an unoccupied house and set up my base there. Then I summoned the commanding officer of the Italians. I said to him. Look here, I don't want any trouble with you lot. I might be on my own,

but I have back up. The RAF will support me. They
are in Alexandria. It's not far away.

So John Pyke, a lone Englishman, set up shop in Pigadia
reporting on German shipping and aircraft movements. I
have no idea if he felt afraid while he carried out his duties.
Somehow I doubt it, but the times were very tense. There
were 35,000 Italian and 10,000 German troops on Rhodes,
a six hour journey away by *caique* and Karpathos had an
airfield and was strategically important.

Locally the Italian discipline had begun to break down.
Women had been assaulted and some families had been
evicted from their own houses. The Italian regime was
growing ever more oppressive. The Italians had been con-
fiscating food from the locals and hoarding it for their possible retreat to Italy. They had control of the windmills and
levied a tithe on what was brought in to be milled. 10, 20
or 30% was taken from every sack of wheat, corn and barley
in this way.

One unexpected consequence was the revival of the use
of hand mills by people in the North of the island. These
were small enough to be hidden and some were hundreds
of years old. Neither the German nor the Italian armies
were fully mechanised in the Second War. Even when
Germany invaded Russia they used thousands of horses for
transportation. For every ten horses used, another was
needed to transport fodder and so on. Preparing to leave,
the Italians began to hoard livestock as well as food and
confiscated mules and donkeys from the villages. These
were beasts of burden and of transport and their loss
caused considerable hardship. Some had been in the same
family for many years.

I ask John how the locals treated him.

Wonderful. If they had bread they would share it with
you. Not half. They would give you three quarters.

We sit silent for a while and I wonder how to tell my friends on Karpathos about this man and if anyone remembered him. The situation in the Dodecanese deteriorated rapidly for the allies and following the failure of Churchill's Dodecanese Campaign the Germans came to Karpathos in September 1943. There was some resistance from the Italians, but they were not combat troops and the Germans were heavily armed. John had to leave and was despatched with a small detachment of men to Ikaria. He related to me what he thought was a funny incident. Early one morning in November 1943 at Agios Kirikos, the port of Ikaria, he had just got off to sleep when the local school teacher woke him up:

> *Figete, figete, prepei na figete. Grigora.* Go, go, you have to leave fast.

He looked out of the window to see a German battle cruiser entering harbour. He could hear the anchor tumbling into the sea as he got dressed. Up he went, over the mountain behind where he had been staying. Some villagers stopped him and explained the Italians had confiscated all the food and had locked it up in a big store at Perdiki. He laughs as he tells me:

> There were 4 Italians with rifles guarding Perdiki. I waved my revolver around and they did not put up much resistance. So we liberated the food. The Ikarians were very happy.

John is tired now and a little confused. I say I have to leave and he invites me back.

The next time I go he digs some papers out for me, trusting me with his precious records.

It would seem that John had a fair old time in the area. He helped capture Kastellorizo and Symi and came back to Karpathos twice. The Germans retreated from Karpathos in late 1944 and on 8th November John set himself up as the representative of an Imperial power, Great Britain. Based in the Italian court and administrative building that still stands in Pigadia he set about organising food distribution, police, health, justice and so on. The people of the village still remember British officers arriving with sacks of beautiful white flour as well as biscuits and cloth for making clothes. But life was very hard. John recorded a *caique* loaded with starving and dead refugees sent from Rhodes because the Germans could not feed the population for which they were responsible.

The end of the Second World war in Europe came at one minute past midnight on 8th may 1945. The German armies in the Dodecanese wanted to capitulate and John was sent to Rhodes to accept their surrender. He set off in a small *caique*, sailing through the night with three colleagues, only to find that the Royal Navy had arrived and taken charge. In the dark the captain of the *caique* was blinded by a searchlight from a Royal Navy ship and there was a collision:

Not much damage done.

said John with a lift to his voice and the hint of a smile. John Pyke was sent from Rhodes to take charge of Kalymnos and remained there until 5th September 1945. He was mentioned in despatches twice. I am sure he deserved more. John Pyke, was an officer and a gentleman. And a very, very nice man.

What makes you happy

Villagers are well aware of their strengths and often aware of their weaknesses. One joke they wryly tell about themselves is as follows:

God had three wishes to give to the world. He chose a German, an American and a villager from *to chorio*.

He asked the German:

What do you wish for?

The German answered:

My neighbour has a new Mercedes Benz SUV. I want one just like it.

God waved his hand in a dramatic gesture and there was a beautiful new Mercedes Benz SUV. He turned to the American:

What do you wish for?

The American thought for a while, then told God:

I have a humble home, but my neighbour has a new, colonial style, five bedroom house with a lawn at the front and a pool at the back. I want the same.

A majestic wave of God's arm and there it was: a new, colonial style, five bedroomed house with a lawn at the front and a pool at the back.

God turned to the villager and asked what would make him happy. The villager, thought for a while and explained:

I have a good life, I have children and grandchildren and my health is fine. The only thing is that my goat gives very little milk though my neighbour's goat gives plenty.

God was pleased with the modesty of the man and asked gently if he wanted a goat like his neighbour's. The villager considered this carefully, then replied:

No. Please kill his goat.

Windmills

The people of the village leave few monuments to their lives: only the olive groves and terraces and a scattering of small white chapels and mills. There are upwards of 60 windmills in the north of the Island and Saria and 14 watermills. Their age has yet to be accurately determined 'though documentation dates back to at least 1700 and it is likely some are medieval. The mills appear to be influenced by Venetian design and construction: with squat, round fronted, elegant, sculptured forms that appear to be of simple construction until you consider the size of the shaft and take into account the massive forces that would be exerted by the flimsy sails when powered by strong winds.

I have met one man who claims he can build windmills and know several who can repair them. An English archaeologist, Holly, fell in love with these mills and it is because of her that we know something of their history. Each mill belongs to a different family and are often owned by the firstborn daughters. Some are owned by younger daughters as several rich fathers built 2 or 3 mills so that their other daughters could have a dowry. Some are owned by men of course, and occasionally they are sold. They were used regularly into the 1960's and then the Prearis family introduced a diesel driven, mechanical mill and the windmills' working days were over. This mechanical mill does not have any air of romance about it, but inside are the same millstones and on the wall, in pencil, are scribbled notes from half a century ago:

Iannis Karellas owes 72 *drachmes* for 12 bags, Fortini
another 30 *drachmes*...

and it is possible to reconstruct the old village life once
again. Iannis is my neighbour and when I asked if he had
paid the bill he told me:

Oh yes, many years ago.

Strangely while exploring mills with Holly I gained some
insight into medieval English country life. There was one
water mill that Holly wanted to explore. Below Olymbos on
the valley bed it was in perfect condition, but the owner,
Michaeli, was reticent to open it up. We went to see him
together and he laughed and joked to his wife as he took
down the key from the wall of his bar. Clearly there was
something ribald going on, but I could not penetrate the
dialect. We were all very professional as we explored the
elegant, vernacular construction. Inside, we learned how
the machinery worked and took measurements of the pad-
dles and chutes and millstones.

After a while, in the dark, I noticed a chimney and an al-
cove about the size of a small bed. I asked Michaeli if he
kept a fire here and he told me yes and laughed, telling me
it was a nice place in the winter to come with his wife to
work, but he was laughing so much he could't finish the
sentence. Slowly, I understood something of village life.
Traditional houses here are very small, with no heating.
Most have only one or two rooms and one large *sofa,* or
bed, in which parents and children slept all together.
Clearly the mill offered a place for the adults to escape to
when they were married, and from what I could understand, from before they were married. And the Miller's Tale
from Chaucer came to mind with its jokes and innuendos.

In the old days there was no privacy to be had and sex
in the open air might sound romantic, but is rarely com-

fortable, especially in winter. Shepherds with their crude shelters did not stand a chance. Owning a mill offered more than wealth: it offered privacy and status and opportunity with the opposite sex. Who could resist a handsome man with a warm fire on a cold winters day? I hinted that I understood and Michaeli laughed and Chaucer winked.

Old Boats

Twenty years ago the airport in the south could only cope with small aircraft from Rhodes and the road was a gravel and mud track, so everything and everybody came by sea, either from Rhodes or from Athens. Diafani had no harbour in those days and no matter the weather, the ferry boats would pause out at sea and small craft would go out to fetch passengers and cargo. In wild seas this could be a hazardous operation and there were some close calls but, despite one or two falling into the sea, no passengers were lost.

Without a harbour, the village was open to the weather and suffered badly in southeasterly and south winds and because it lacked a sheltered anchorage we were forever hauling boats out of the sea and up the beach or off the beach and into the sea. This was arduous, but fun: co-operation was required and whenever people in the village work together there are plenty of jokes. I used to share an old boat, the Marina, with friends in the village. For years I had wanted a small fibreglass boat to go to the beaches, so when Nikos called me I was excited:

Is it a small boat?

Well not exactly.

What do you mean?

About 6 metres!

Is it fibreglass?

Well not exactly.

???

It's made of wood.

This is Greece and you never get exactly what you want, but a six metre wooden boat is heavy and difficult to handle; it used to take half a dozen of us to drag it into the sea after a storm and twice as many to pull it up the beach again when the weather threatened. But manpower was not the only problem. As captain you need to have a certain amount of courage and some status and I am not endowed with either. You don't want to drag a heavy boat out of the sea unless there really is a storm coming.

In Greece that means the storm has started, the wind is howling and the sea is pounding the beach: so you wait in the *cafeneion*, watch the sea and hope the storm will go away. If it doesn't you announce to whoever is listening that you are going to get your boat, you walk slowly down the beach, look at the boat and take the measure of the waves while you summon the courage to act. Slowly, very slowly, you take off your shoes and maybe your trousers, take the rope attached to the prow, pull the boat towards you and carefully leap onto half a ton of bucking vessel.

If you perform this manoeuvre without damaging yourself too much, you get the oars ready, stand in the stern, row backwards and haul on the heavy anchor. If you are lucky the anchor comes up without snagging on rocks or another anchor. Now you stand and row slowly along the beach towards the *cafeneion*, trying to maintain composure, but still attract attention. After a while, someone may look up and if that someone is a friend, that friend will alert the other men to the fact you need help. Slowly they assemble on the shore where the beach is not too steep. On their way they pick up assorted bits of wood, *fallangi*, around one metre long. They place the *fallangi* up the beach like railway sleepers parallel to the sea and at right angles to the boat. Meanwhile, a few metres off shore, you stand and use the oars to balance the boat against the wind and the waves. When the men are ready you wait for a large wave, the men shout and you row rapidly and surf towards the beach. You hit the beach at right angles, run to the prow, stand there a second to throw the rope to the men, leap onto the beach (or into the sea if you have screwed up), turn round, lift up the prow and with your bare foot push the first *fallangi* into the sea and under the keel. With a whooup the men take the strain and heave so that your heavy, wooden boat slides across the *fallangi* a few centimetres from your toes and up the beach. Now you take the gunnels. Whooup. Another metre up the beach. Whooup. Another and on until you and the men feel the sea will come no further and the boat is safe. You prop up the boat, tidy the oars away, find your shoes if you are lucky, put on your trousers and wander to the *cafeneion* where thanks are waved away and offers of coffee are refused and the men return to dozing.

Wooden boats take a long time to stop under weigh and you have to think in advance or you will collide with one boat or another, or hit the pier or damage a swimmer or two. A heavy boat needs a heavy anchor with a heavy chain and you need a lot of muscle to lower it into the water and pull it back into the boat again. You also need strength to row a boat like this: each oar is four metres long and it is difficult to make headway against even a light breeze.

My first job, after I changed my life, was to transport two men and twenty bags of goat shit down the coast to Papa Minas beach. It was a calm day, which was fortunate, as we only had ten centimetres of freeboard. I was not expected to unload the sacks, but I had to clean the boat of dried goat pellets. The work took four hours and I was paid

10,000 *drachmes* (20 euros) and three litres of petrol. An Albanian's wage, I was told in the *cafeneion* and earned myself the epithet, *O Arbanos*.

For years I thought the proper name for such boats was *barca*. Now I have learned that they are *maounas* and they used to be built in the village. There were many such boats in the days when the only land transport was by mule or donkey and *maounas* formed the backbone of the local transport system. They had sails, but could not sail against the wind and so the old people, men and women, rowed and rowed and rowed. Going to Palatia in the summer could take five or six hours. On arrival the people walked up the canyon to Argos to collect freshly milled flour, figs, goats cheese, goats, or maybe a grandmother or some children and then back down to Palatia to sail back to the village in a stiff breeze: *maestros* or *trasmontana*. In Diafani they unloaded their cargo on the little mole, perhaps setting off again, rowing north to repeat the performance. The optimum crew numbered four: each position in the boat had its own name, and each crew member was a specialist in that position. Sometimes they would row or sail to Pigadia and back to sell their produce. The journey took all day. Undeterred by bad weather, the old captains would keep *gialo gialo*, close to the coast, if there was a storm from the north in the summer, or calmly ride the big breakers when the *sirocco* came in winter time.

Maounas were used for fishing and each one was capable of carrying hundreds of metres of nets. During the war the Germans confiscated fishing nets to stop the men fishing at night so the men fished in the daytime with dynamite removed from unexploded bombs. In previous times there were plenty of fish. *Sharpa* are very tasty, white fish, nearly first class in price, but even diving I rarely see a big one. One old man told me that one very hot summer's day he and his brother went fishing and came across a huge shoal of *sharpa* travelling slowly through the water with their noses showing above the surface. Two explosions and they had enough to fill their boat, a thousand or more of one kilo fish, maybe a tonne in all. These people are hunters and gatherers: in times of plenty they share and hope that in hard times their generosity will be remembered. There were no freezers in those days and with too many fish to sell they gave them away to all and sundry in Diafani, before loading mules and travelling to Olymbos to distribute the rest. Sometimes they received a coffee or string of onions in return. That night they told stories and shared *ouzos*.

During the Second World War, after the Germans took over from the Italians, four men from the village sailed to Turkey in a small boat. Their parents used to do this journey to work in Asia Minor before the Greco-Turkish war of 1919-1922 and the exchange of populations in 1923, but these men could not go direct. They hid in caves and behind capes in the daytime and rowed and sailed at night: steering by the stars and the silhouettes of vaguely remembered islands. The voyage took three days and nights. Of course they were detained in Turkey, but used their contacts to get a message to the British Embassy:

> Beware, the Italians have gone, but the Germans are
> in Karpathos.

One of my favourite boats in the village is a *barca* about 4 metres long. Seemingly held together by paint it is now owned by Iannis, but used to belong to a giant of a man called Ballanos. A war hero, Ballanos lived to a very old age and I remember him going fishing in his late eighties: one eye gone due to a beating in the war and the other eye supported by pebble thick glasses. Ballanos would row out to the horizon in calm seas, sometimes accompanied by an old friend of similar vintage: their combined age was close to 180 years. In windy weather Ballanos would haul this little boat up the beach without assistance, then detach the outboard, weighing 32 kilos, put it over his shoulder and, with the aid of a walking stick carry it home 800 metres up the hill, without stopping.

These days I have a small fibreglass boat *O Erimitis*, the Hermit, powered by a 15 hp Tohatsu outboard motor. As long as I keep to the east side of the islands she is safe in almost any sea: I have dealt with three metre waves and force 7 Beaufort winds and survived. So far. The old Marina is a wreck, she lies on the land past the oven on the way to the harbour: unkempt, unloved, and laying on her side, the wood slowly dries and the colours are bleached. As the wood crumbles, the memories fade, but she was a faithful boat and I am sad to see her demise.

Rembetika

For more than a week the weather had been strange: there was no wind, the sea was calm and in the evenings both sea and sky were the colour of mercury. One afternoon I went fishing for *palamida*, a member of the tuna family; the system is to travel far from the coast to deep water, then slowly trawl a line with feathers and hidden hooks that resemble small squid.

If you are lucky enough to come across a shoal of *palamida* it is possible to catch several at a time: on a line with 13 hooks Georgos once caught 12 fish. Getting them into the boat without snaring yourself or making a birds nest of the line is not easy. That day the clouds lay low and alone in a small boat on a flat sea a long way from land I became paranoid and kept looking around as if something was there and suddenly there was: a dark line in the water stretched out like an oily rope around 20 metres long. It could have been a huge sea snake, a sea monster, basking shark or whale.

At first I was frightened, but fortunately I have seen such a thing before and knew it to be a pod of lazy dolphins. There were five or six of them: the first one steering and the one at the end swimming to push the pod along, while the ones in the middle slept or read a paperback, or did whatever dolphins do when they are taking it easy. They were peaceful, but far out at sea I was apprehensive and, just in case, did not go too close. With dolphins around there would be no *palamida*, so I made the long journey home. That night I ate pasta.

The following night I went fishing again, this time hunting for barracuda by trawling a single lure close to the coast. I was lucky and caught a fair sized fish: enough for two or three of us. Back on land as the light faded, clouds gathered and reflected pink on the silver sea. I sat quietly in the Rahati while Elias grilled the fish. A *parea* developed. Four or five of us with beers and retsina and *meze* and then the fish. By the time it was dark we were joined by Iannis, a coastguard with an earring (!) but only when off duty. New to the village he fits in well. Serious about his work and serious about his fun he is an accomplished musician, playing the *bouzouki* and singing *Rembetika* songs. One of the *parea* was Memo, a fine name for a nostalgic old man. Soon there was talk of the masters of this music, sometimes called the Greek blues, then there were songs of hashish and poverty, exile and loss, written or recorded by Vamvakari and Tsitsanis, Papayoannou and Dalaras. Both Iannis and Memo have good voices and the songs rang out as the bottles clinked and the tears flowed. Any Greek *glendi* has a gamut of feelings and we were taken on a roller coaster of tears and laughter, love and hate, peace and revenge.

By midnight I had drunk enough and I found my way home to the sound of 1920's Smyrna; storm clouds were gathering and there was spectacular thunder and lightning, though very little rain. Of course the electricity shut down, but at Rahati, lit by candles, memories and imagination the party continued until dawn. All this was unplanned and spontaneous. Strangely as I picked my way through the wreckage of the morning I discovered there had been a party at the other end of the village. Gabriella, Andoni and Michaeli combining to host another *glendi* until dawn. Perhaps it was the weather. Then the rain came and I learned, once again, that a litre of retsina for a man of my age is far too much.

The bird I am most familiar with is the Eleanora's Falcon, *falco eleanorae*, a medium sized falcon that comes to us from Madagascar. They arrive each spring around mid April, following northbound, migrating passerines and eating well. Named after Eleanora di Arboria (1350-1404), a Sardinian judge and heroine, who admired these birds so much she passed laws to protect them and incorporated them into her crest, they are to be found along the tumbling mountains north of the village.

Passing by in my boat, late in the day, I sometimes pause in the evening glimmer beneath the enormous sea cliffs where they roost. They know me and are not phased by my presence, but greet me with their plaintive cry: *kek, kek, kek*. Eleanora's are the most elegant fliers and I sit and watch their slim, dark shapes whirl and fall and climb and turn against the pale sky as their cruel, yellow beaks and cheeky white bibs catch the fading sunlight filtering horizontally across the dark mountains.

What do these birds mean to me? Freedom, savagery, skill, beauty? I cannot say, but certainly fun, as they clearly enjoy flying and so would I. The dialect name for these birds is *mavropetritis*, black peregrine, an apt description. They jump from their high ledges, gather speed as they open their wings and fall to the sea before coming out of the dive and up and over into the evening breeze to fly up the face of the cliff and over the top. All this movement without one beat of their wings as they balance two forces of nature: gravity and the wind. In June Eleanora's begin to pair off. I watch as males chase females, competing to fly close to their fancy and close to the sea. At more than 100 kph they skim the waves until the female choses the best flier, they enter into a partnership and hunt and fly together.

In late July and August, eggs are laid in scraps of dried vegetation on ledges and fissures in the cliffs. The young hatch in September, and are still in their nests when small migrating birds heading south provide food for the fledglings and their parents. At dusk the roost spreads out across the sea, forming a net several kilometres over the water, each adult bird quartering 100 metres or more of airspace horizontally and vertically.

The migrating birds time their arrival from the north and east to be in the dark and they flutter close to the sea to avoid being seen. Sometimes they settle on my boat petrified and shivering, ducking down, as hunting Eleanora's skim along the surface. When rested the little birds set off again, frantically zig-zagging in the dark to the rocks and the safety of the night. Occasionally on calm mornings I see pitiful bunches of feathers littering the sea: evidence of the evening's carnage. Young Eleanora's are taught to fly by adults who chase them up the face of the cliffs then down, down, down till they skim the sea and up and over once more; a game to ensure they find a mate next spring and catch little birds when they come again in the autumn; a magic, eternal cycle.

Elenora's stay with us until late October or November when most of them travel south to Crete, then Egypt, where they follow the Nile to Ethiopia, cross the highlands to the Indian Ocean and fly down the coast to Madagascar. Do they remember me as I remember them? This is not a fanciful question: I had a collision with a swallow in a barn in Wales once and from then on, for two summers, on its return from Africa, it would screech and scream every time it saw me. Eleanora's probably see this strange man in a small boat as part of the scenery. Perhaps when I am gone they will miss me. For a while.

The Defining Moment

I do not know what day of the week it was, or even what year, but the time was between six and seven in the evening on a late summer's day. I was in my little boat, half way up the east coast of Saria. I was waiting for Georgos, the sea was rough and it was windy. Those were the days before I became a diver. I had been several hours fishing with *kathetei*, the long, vertical, line with several hooks, catching *perka* and *hanos*: low grade fish that make rich soup. It had not been a good day, but I had enough fish for a meal and now I was going to pick up Georgos who had been diving all afternoon. He was north of Sta Maria, a wild place with steep cliffs and more than 20 metres of water.

I was burned by the sun, tired and cold and hungry, but Georgos did not want to come into the boat. He never does. When his blood is up for hunting, he hunts. Down, up, down, up again, spearing fish, feeding them onto the line, looking around, searching for the big one, the big fish. Three deep breaths and down again 20, 25 or 30 metres, squeezing under this rock, pulling himself into that cave, hunting the big, valuable fish. He came to the surface. I shouted at him to come in the boat and he shouted back. It was my boat, but I could not leave him there so moved round the cape a little to get out of the worst of the wind and wait and wait and wait. It was nearly dark when he let me pick him up. First the spear guns come into the boat, the *pendaraena*, with five points and then the single spear for clean shots on big fish. After that, my job is to pull in the fish: each one threaded carefully on the line attached to

the balloon. For him it was a good day, there were several
groupers, a couple of octopus, *scarroi* and *sargoi* and for
our supper a nice *kefalos*. Georgos waited in the water to
help me lift the fish into the boat without causing them
damage. I was pissed off that I had had to wait so long, but
did not say anything since there were only a few more days
before I returned to the UK. Georgos came into the boat as
only he can: a big man he rises up out of the sea like a seal
and somehow twists to sit on the edge of the boat, a black,
beatific, barrel of a man:

Start the engine.

he told me and turned around to face me with water
streaming from his wet-suit and great globules of snot running down his face. I started the engine and set off south. I
don't wear shoes in the boat, not even *sayonaras*: in a small
boat in wild weather I have to use every sense to assay the
sea and guess its actions. Water was sloshing around the
bottom of the boat and I was nearly up to my ankles in
blood and scales and the guts of dead and nearly dead fish.
I looked up at Georgos' snotty face and started to laugh. I
laughed and laughed and laughed and laughed. Georgos
tried to ask why. I couldn't tell him, just laughed some
more so that he joined in and we were laughing together:
two helpless loons in a small boat in a large sea. I had been
thinking about my other life, the one in civilisation: the
family, the terraced house, the job, the money, the secretary, the chauffeur driven car. It was impossible to explain,
so we just carried on laughing. Approaching Steno with its
strong currents and wild sea I waved my arms at the grey,
lumpy water and finally managed to say:

What the fuck am I doing here?

A question I have been asking myself ever since. The pair of us collapsed again in helpless giggles and the die was cast.

Lightning Source UK Ltd.
Milton Keynes UK
UKOW041352161012

200662UK00001B/5/P